THE SCRI

Borgo Press Books by S. Fowler Wright

Arresting Delia: An Inspector Cleveland Classic Crime Novel
The Attic Murder: An Inspector Combridge & Mr. Jellipot Classic Crime Novel
*The Bell Street Murders: An Inspector Combridge & Mr. Jellipot Classic Crime
    Novel*
Beyond the Rim: A Lost Race Fantasy
Black Widow: A Classic Crime Novel
The Capone Caper: Mr. Jellipot vs. the King of Crime: A Classic Crime Novel
Crime & Co.: An Inspector Cleveland Classic Crime Novel
Dawn: A Novel of Global Warming
Dead by Saturday: An Inspector Cleveland Classic Crime Novel
Dream; or, The Simian Maid: A Fantasy of Prehistory (Marguerite Cranleigh #1)
Elfwin: An Historical Novel
The End of the Mildew Gang: An Inspector Cauldron Classic Crime Novel (Mil-
    dew Gang #3)
*Four Callers in Razor Street: An Inspector Combridge & Mr. Jellipot Classic
    Crime Novel*
The Hanging of Constance Hillier: An Inspector Cleveland Classic Crime Novel
The Hidden Tribe: A Lost Race Fantasy
*The Jordans Murder: An Inspector Combridge & Mr. Jellipot Classic Crime
    Novel*
The King Against Anne Bickerton: A Classic Crime Novel
The Mildew Gang: An Inspector Cauldron Classic Crime Novel (Mildew Gang
    #1)
*Murder in Bethnal Square: An Inspector Combridge & Mr. Jellipot Classic Crime
    Novel*
The Police and the Public
*Post-Mortem Evidence: An Inspector Combridge & Mr. Jellipot Classic Crime
    Novel*
The Return of the Mildew Gang: An Inspector Cauldron Classic Crime Novel
    (Mildew Gang #2)
*The Rissole Mystery: An Inspector Combridge & Mr. Jellipot Classic Crime
    Novel*
The Screaming Lake: A Lost Race Fantasy
*The Secret of the Screen: An Inspector Combridge & Mr. Jellipot Classic Crime
    Novel*
Spiders' War: A Novel of the Far Future (Marguerite Cranleigh #3)
Three Witnesses: A Classic Crime Novel
*Too Much for Mr. Jellipot: An Inspector Combridge & Mr. Jellipot Classic Crime
    Novel*
The Vengeance of Gwa: A Fantasy of Prehistory (Marguerite Cranleigh #2)
Was Murder Done? A Classic Crime Novel
Who Murdered Reynard? A Classic Crime Novel
*The Wills of Jane Kanwhistle: An Inspector Combridge & Mr. Jellipot Classic
    Crime Novel*
*With Cause Enough?: An Inspector Combridge & Mr. Jellipot Classic Crime
    Novel*

THE SCREAMING LAKE

A Lost Race Fantasy

by

S. FOWLER WRIGHT

THE BORGO PRESS

An Imprint of Wildside Press LLC

MMIX

CONTENTS

PART ONE

PART TWO

PART ONE

CHAPTER ONE

A STRANGER TO MANAOS

DEVEREUX sat at one of the small round tables that were at the rear end of the cafe and endeavoured to eat as though he were both unhurried and unconcerned, though his heart beat at times in a way that was hard to still. He thought, with some doubtful confidence, of the revolver his pocket held, and with less satisfaction of the fact that the short twilight was near, and that he would have to return to his hotel through streets which would have no more light than would come from the tropic moon.

The man he had knocked down sat with his three companions at one of the larger tables nearer the door. His left hand at times would rub a reddened cheekbone; his right would feel the haft of his knife in a furtively restless way. The girl, at the sound of whose screams Devereux had so foolishly interfered, sat on the knee of the man further away, a loose-limbed angular man, very black of hair and eyes, and with a sun-darkened mahogany skin. Like the others, she glanced across the room at him at times, but with dislike rather than any gratitude in the curiosity of her bold, contemptuous eyes. He wondered whether it would be a signal for their attack if he should rise, and move to the door. Or was his fear that of a nervous stranger, who exaggerated the perils of foreign streets? Was it more likely that they would scowl at him, and let him go? Or would they follow till they could close around him in a quiet place, and make an end of him which none would see? Or perhaps use their knowledge of the town to go ahead, and ambush him from a shadowed porch, with a sudden rush, or no need of more than a well-thrown knife?

9

He felt, in imagination, the sharp blade sink into his neck. He staggered forward while he strove to hold in the blood with impotent hands. He fell, gaining oblivion as rough hands tore at his pockets to take the spoils that the victors claim.... It was foolish to sit here, while the shadows lengthened outside. It was cowardice to delay to test the event. Or should he speak to the proprietor at the bar (an ill-favoured man, but whose rapid curses had held them back from him before), asking if he could telephone for protection from the police?

It might be wise, but he knew it was what he would never do. It might make him look a most utter fool! No, he would sit there while his courage went, but he must rise at last, to face that which could be proved in no other way.

Whatever his fears might invent, there was one thing which he did not mistake. They were still looking at him, and he was sure that he engaged their thoughts and that he was the subject of some disputation among them, in which it seemed that the man who was nursing the girl urged something upon the others which they did not quickly accept, though his gesture was that of one who had authority, or advantage of status over those others to whom he spoke.

It was even as Devereux resolved to test the peril in which he stood that the man tipped the girl somewhat casually from his lap, and came over to the little table at which he sat.

He pulled out a chair for his own use, and sat down unasked. "I tell Pedro," he said, "that you are a stranger for all to see. You are of Europe, not here. You have not our ways. The girl is a sly thief, who would be better for harder blows. But in Manaos we have easy ways. Will you drink with me, that they may see that the thing is done?"

Devereux looked at a man whom he could not like, but who spoke better words than he had expected to hear. His appearance did not encourage confidence. In London he would have been one to avoid, a man self-advertised of the criminal class. But the standards of Manaos were doubtless different, and must be learnt by one who sought to thrive in a strange land.

The man did not appear to be lacking in intelligence. He had had the sense to use slow clear words, so that he had been easy to understand. Devereux, whose Portuguese had been learned in an Oxford Street language-school, and who had landed at Rio no more than three weeks before, was still puzzled by rapid speech, though he had been told that he had mastered the language well.

He might distrust the character of the man who sat opposite to him, or the sincerity of the goodwill that his words implied, but it would he foolish to show any sign of doubt. If peace could be bought at the price of a drink, it would be little to pay.

He signalled to a waiter who had approached in a diffident manner, as though being as uncertain as Devereux himself of the purpose with which he had been accosted. The man said no more till his glass was filled, when he raised it with a courteous gesture. "Señor," he said, "I am Manuel Fonseca, at your service. I drink to your prosperity in a pleasant land."

They were amicable, and very apposite words. It was prosperity which Devereux sought, as a man must who finds himself an outcast from his own country, and obliged to look for a new foothold of life in lands where he will be hard to follow, and which must therefore be hardly tolerable to man. Also, he re-minded himself, he must not refuse opportunity to make acquaintance of other men, if he were to explore the possibilities of these outliers of civilisation to which he came. The blend of caution and enterprise that was in the mixed ancestry of his blood ruled his reply.

"Señor," he said, "my name is Devereux Carsholt. I am English, as you may have guessed, and a stranger, as it was easy for you to see. If I blundered, will you do me the great favour to express my regret to Señor Pedro in better words than I should be able to choose?"

He spoke with an inward doubt of how this apology would be received. Was it deficient in the words of courtesy which were so freely used in this land, and in excess of the meaning they seemed to bear? Might it not be a fresh offence to ask Fonseca to be the medium of their transmission? Was it a case where a gift of money would be considered a more appropriate solatium for a bruised head? Or perhaps a more deadly affront? Looking at Pedro, it might be though that such a man could have little sensitiveness to wounds, and little honour to lose. But that was to judge him by English standards, on which it would be unsafe to rely.

But whether appropriate or not, the apology was graciously received.

"Señor, they see us drink. It is done. Do you come to Manaos, may I ask, of pleasure, or for business affairs?"

"I have no business here. I am looking round."

"It is a land where there is much to see. It is so near the unknown."

"I have been told that the Amazon had now been traversed many times for its whole length, and that there are stations along its banks."

"Many times? It is less than that. But the river, and its great branches, yes. There is Iquitos, which is no less than a town. You will have come nine hundred miles from Rio to here. You will go thirteen hundred more, and you will come to Iquitos, which has a pier. There you might find a cargo-boat from your own land lying tied to the quay. You may say the great rivers are known, but if you go ten miles in the forests to right or left you will be in an unknown land which you will be first to see, though I do not say you will see far."

"I suppose the growth is too dense?"

"So you will find. But beyond that? Men may suppose it the same. Yet they may make no more than a bad guess. It is unknown for a million miles."

"A million miles?" Devereux found it hard to control the incredulity of his voice, though he was helped thereto by a prudent doubt of whether Manuel might not be aiming to pick a quarrel with him, the cause of which would have a better sound than that he had interfered to protect a loud-screaming girl. Was he to be led to make remarks disparaging to Brazil, and then to be beaten up, if not worse, by patriotic Manaos citizens, who could not endure the English stranger's supercilious contempt of their native soil?

But Manuel showed no sign of offence. "A million miles?" he replied. "Yes. I do not mean stretched in a straight line. I mean square. A million square miles of an unvisited land. There is more than that. You could cut that out, and there would yet be a great country remaining. In such a space there must be wonders we do not know!"

"I have supposed," Devereux replied, "that it is all a dense, hot forest, level and low, which becomes swamp when the rains fall, or at the melting of the snow in the great mountains in which its rivers begin."

"That is the common guess. It is little more. Is it likely that what we see on the river's bank will go on and on for so great a space? Is not the earth made in another way, changing ever its face

12

as the miles extend? If I were not tied here as I am, I would seek that which may be as strange as Columbus found."

"But there must be many who are not tied. If it be as you say, which I do not doubt"—the last words were spoken in hurried correction, lest there might be an opportunity for resentment in those that had gone before—"why do they not explore the wonders of this great land which is theirs, and from which wealth might be won which is hard to guess?"

Fonseca cast his hands apart in a gesture which was new to Devereux, but easy to understand. "Señor, it is plain to see that you have come to a land that you do not know. It is tomorrow, always it is tomorrow with us. If we have food in store, or money to buy a meal, or bananas grown on a small patch, we are hard to stir. We would lie in the sun. In the evening, we spear a fish, or it may be two. Why, there are settlements on the river banks that are short of food, though the soil will give them three crops a year, and there are fish to catch, and in the forest are many creatures to shoot or snare.

"They clear small patches to plant, and lie about as men whose work is soon done, and the forest, that does not rest either night or day, overgrows and chokes them again. They play no more than a game that the forest wins."

"Yet I have been told that the work is hard in the rubber plantations that are farther up the river?"

"So it is. But they are Indians working there. It is so hard that they die. It is no work for us who have whiter blood. Yet you will understand that they die. It is a land where men make little effort to do more than their mouths require; and, being driven, they die.... Why even the great treasure of Ixitol, the place of which is set down on a map which may be inspected by all who will, has been unclaimed for three hundred years."

"I suppose there are many tales of buried treasure which are either ill-founded, or hard to locate?"

"So there are. But that of Ixitol is of a different kind, nor do I know that it was said to be buried at all. But if you would become rich in an easy way, you should go to the Library of San José, where the map is open to all. If you ask of Señor Amerigo, the librarian there, he will tell you that which is no less true because it took place on a distant day, and you may think his words to be more weighty than mine."

Devereux thanked him politely for this information, but put the idea aside with a smile such as most men would give to so vague a tale. He said, with reason, that treasure-seeking of any kind was for those who knew the country better than he.

Señor Fonseca approved a prudent reply. He said it was not to be expected that strangers would attempt that which the natives were disposed to avoid. Life was different in the days when Peixoto lived, by whom the treasure was found. He could look back on Cortes and Pizarro, and a score of other adventurers in untrodden ways, as men who were scarcely dead, and whose spirits brooded over the land. Emptying his glass, Fonseca rose, and with sufficient courtesies of leave-taking returned to the table where his companions were still seated.

Devereux, vaguely puzzled though he was, had lost the fear of immediate violence or ambush which had possessed him before. He rose also, and passed out to the wide, untidy street upon which the darkness already fell. As he swung open the door, he looked sideways at the seated group. He saw that Pedro's eyes were following him with a malevolent glance, that had yet the satisfied look of one who had found the revenge he sought. The girl was again on Fonseca's knee, and he could see no more of her than the back of a head of hair that curled, glossy, abundant, black, and bedecked with draggled and dying flowers.

Why, he asked himself, had he entered so dubious a door? Well, the meals at his highly-recommended hotel had seemed to him to be neither wholesome nor very cleanly prepared. And, when one is wandering about, it is better to go out than to stay inside. He had no better reason than that.

He could not hear Fonseca say, as the door closed: "He would not show he was caught, but he bit—he bit. He will fix the hook in his gills. You may count him dead in an evil way, and one for which there will be no charges to us, nor any questions to turn aside."

"So it may be," Pedro grumbled, feeling his cheek-bone again, "but it would have been better to see him die."

CHAPTER TWO

AMERIGO TELLS AN UNLIKELY TALE

THE heat was not very great. In the Amazon valley it seldom is, as it is seldom cool. It is a land where sunstroke is never known. But for four midday hours Manaos sleeps in the sun.

It was three-fifteen, and Manaos was barely stretching itself awake for the hours of the afternoon, which would be busy enough, for it is a place of commerce, and loaded wharves, standing where rivers meet, and gathering the grudging tribute the forest pays for two thousand ascending miles.

Devereux, having become impatient for a call which he felt it would be foolish to make, came down a wide white street that was still empty of more life than a drowsing dog, between buildings some of which were substantial enough in the newest styles that Southern Europe prefers, and others little better than iron-roofed sheds, until he came to the library of San José, where he had resolved to enquire concerning the treasure Peixoto found, not as a matter with which he would have further concern, but so that he should be able to think of more practical things.

It was not sense that there should be public knowledge for three hundred years of a great treasure that no man took, or that he, a stranger to the unknown land and its difficult ways, should be able to win that which those who knew more would not attempt. Men were too keen on treasure for that!

In fact, it was this bizarre quality of the tale which had been most potent to vex his mind. He thought at times that Manuel Fonseca (a man it was most easy to doubt) had caught him with foolish talk, making game of one whose ignorance invited a jest. But he did not think him to be of that kind, but rather one who took life

15

in a serious, though it might also be a sinister mood.... Well, the simplest course was to ask, when there would doubtless be sufficient reason shown to put it out of his mind. He had read tales enough, either invented or true, of treasure shown upon secret maps, which were given by dying hands, or perhaps pilfered from dying men, and would then be cozened from hand to hand by ways of bargain or blood, until men came, by paces and Signs, to a place of bones and a rifled hole. All that was common enough, be it truth or lies. But a tale of treasure the location of which was a public talk, and which no one took...! Well, a librarian should be likely to give a courteous reply to a stranger who would ask in a civil tone, even though the question should have little meaning or none, from a man who had been misled.

Señor Amerigo was a small man, wizened and bald, with a beard trimmed to a point, very white on his walnut skin. He had eyes which were bright and black, denying his years, which could not be few. He walked slowly, with little ease, having the infirmity of shortened and twisted leg.

He received Mr. Carsholt with a formal courtesy that became sincere when he learnt that he was a graduate of an English college, and found that he possessed a better knowledge of Portuguese than most Englishmen can display. The library he controlled was not large, but it contained old and curious books which the early settlers had brought to the land, some of which might not be easily duplicated in the Europe from which they came, and other records, manuscripts and books, that had been produced in the four hundred years that the Portuguese had possessed the coast and the river banks of Brazil, which was little less than they did at the present day. These Señor Amerigo was more than willing to show to anyone with intelligence to appreciate and scholarship to understand what they were; but when Devereux said: "Have you anything which relates to an old treasure that a man named Peixoto is said to have discovered three hundred years back?" his expression changed, as though he had been suddenly asked a question of an unexpectedly personal kind.

"Who," he asked in return, "could have told you of that? It has been mentioned to me but once in the last twenty years, and it meant death then, as I suppose that it ever will."

Devereux saw by this reply that there was at least some truth in Fonseca's tale, and that of a serious kind. "I understood," he replied, "that it was a public matter that all might learn."

16

"So it is. But it is not one which I would show to a friend, or to any I did not hate…. It is by that tale that I walk as I do now, having had great fortune in that, though, at the time, I looked at it another way. But that is long past…. It was no more than two years ago that it took tribute again, which was the evil work of one, Manuel Fonseca, who so had his revenge on a foe that he would not kill in a straighter way, there being some law in this city, from which it would be his ruin to flee, who is merchant here both of known and illicit wares."

Devereux heard a warning in these words he could not miss. Nor could he doubt that Amerigo spoke as a friend. He became frank. "I had the tale from the same mouth."

"It was a probable guess. What harm had you done to him?"

"Nothing at all. I had knocked down a man, Pedro, who kicked a girl. I was most likely a fool. After that, she found a place on Fonseca's knee."

"You were unwise. There are many Pedros in this city. They are common as stones. I cannot say who was the man you struck. But it is clear that Fonseca gave him revenge in a way that would cheat the law. You will be wise if you ask no more."

"I am warned, as you say. I must thank your kindness for that. But it will do no harm if I hear the tale."

"So I must hope. And you appear to be of a stable mind. But men have heard it before who have gone to death though I have warned them, as I am warning you. Do you drink maté?"

"No. No one does in England. Till I landed in Rio I did not know what it was."

"So I have heard. I enquired whether you had learned its use since you landed here."

"No. To be frank, it is a taste I have not sought to acquire."

"Well, you should. It is more potent than tea, and it is said that it is less harmful to drink. But it is a taste you must learn. If you will join me in that, you shall have the tale."

"It would be a small price to pay."

"It is one you must, if you would prosper here. It is drunk of all, high and low. If you refuse it you cannot visit friends or receive. You will make no social progress at all. Beside that, it is better than tea. It will do you good."

Señor Amerigo left an assistant in charge of the library, to which, in fact, no one had entered while this conversation had been carried on, and led the way to his private apartment. Devereux was soon reclining in a siesta chair on a palm-shaded patio gay with a scarlet riot of tropic flowers, while a bare-legged, brown-skinned girl, deft and demure, handed him a carved silver-mounted cup in which there had been put a spoonful of the coarsely-powdered leaves of the maté bush, on to which, after a sprinkle of sugar, scalding water was poured. Señor Amerigo dropped a lighted cinder into his cup, which scorched the sugar and maté powder before the water was poured.

"I do not offer you this," he said, "because it strengthens the flavour, which, being the first time that you taste, you will not prefer; but there will come a time (if you will make Manaos your home, and reflect that those who seek treasure will seldom find more than a quick death and a quiet grave) when you will take it as I do now.... You should drink it at the most heat that your tongue endures."

While he spoke, the girl had handed bombillas—silver tubes with tiny perforated bulbs at their lower ends—through which the maté tea is sucked, as English drinks are drawn through a straw. Devereux tasted that which he did not like, but resolved to swallow without sign of distaste. It was the first tribute he paid to the tale of the treasure Peixoto saw, and if it were more than a small instalment toward the whole he would be a fortunate man.

Stretched in comfort under the palms, Señor Amerigo began his tale.

"Hermes Peixoto," he said, "was a half-breed, the son of a Portuguese sea-captain, a man of noble descent who forsook the sea for the lure of gold in the new-found lands, and of an Indian woman of the Guarani race, whom it is said that he took to wife in a better way than was often done at that time. Hermes was of his father's kind, loving adventure, and restless for changing days and a new sky. He had some education also, for which his father paid, and the Jesuits gave. But he was Indian too, and could go where he would in the lands where the Guarani dwelt, or any tribes that were friendly to them; and as the years passed, and his father died, he would be absent more and more in the savage lands, coming to the settlements only when he would buy powder or salt or what else he might need for his own use, or to barter with the wild Indians of the woods.

"He came back at last with a handful of shining gems which were real enough to bring riches to a cousin who claimed them when he was dead, which was no more than a matter of weeks, for he had

18

been poisoned in a way that no leech of that time could understand, as, indeed, they might be no better now, for there are drugs that the Indians know that are strange to us after four hundred years, and they have secrets they do not sell.

"But the stones were real, and so was the map he made, which is here still.

"And besides that there are many marvellous things which he is said to have told, but he wrote nothing down, only the map. And these tales may have been delusions that poison bred, or they may have been altered by other mouths, so that they may include things which he did not say.

"But some warnings he gave concerning the Indians of the great forests and swamps, which must first be traversed, have since been proved true, such as that of the cannibals who can treat their enemies' heads so that they shrink to five inches or four, while all the features remain; and of the Indians who cover themselves with luminous paint, so that they shine in the dark like monstrous glowworms among the trees.

"But beyond that, only this is soberly sure, that he had the fierce anger of a man who had been brought to death in a treacherous way, so that he strove to incite others to destroy those who had done him so great a wrong.

"He did not wish to conceal the road to the riches he claimed to have found, nor to make profit therefrom. It was revenge he sought, and to start the most men he could on the same track.

"You may suppose that he found those who were glad to hear. Expeditions started almost at once, to be followed by others, some large, some small, each sanguine of success, whatever evil might have befallen the ones before."

"You mean that they have all failed to locate the treasure?" Devereux asked. Remembering that it was said to lie in some remote part of a savage and unknown land which more than equalled Europe in size, that did not sound an improbable result, even though it might be more genuine than the subjects of such traditions most often are.

"No. I cannot say that. It is not certain that they did not arrive. No one knows. The sure fact is that you do not return."

"May they not regain civilisation another way?"

"Which would you suggest? But if they should, would they not be heard of again? And would it happen so every time?"

19

"No. It doesn't sound likely. Though I suppose those who find great wealth may not be anxious to advertise it. They might be glad to slip quietly away, to avoid taxation and other claims."

"So they might—if they could. But I ask again which way could they go that would not be longer and worse than to return by the way they went.

"Besides, if they could find the treasure and bear it away, why should not others have reached the same spot and come back with the tale of a sucked egg? But that is guessing, which all may do as they please; the only fact which is known is that they do not return."

"Have they all started from here?"

"Not at all, the map is in the library here, for it was in the settlement here (which was then the highest upon the river) that Peixoto died. But the best way is from Essabo, which can be reached in two weeks' journey, first up the flood, and then by a smaller river."

"You said you went with one of these expeditions yourself?"

"I started out with one which was well equipped, and very confident that it would not be turned back without finding the place, and whatever treasure there might be, either much or none.

"This was more than twenty years ago, when I was younger, and willing for any chance that would bring experience of strange scenes or events, without greatly caring whether there was any treasure or not.

"It was then about fifteen years since any men had been known to make the attempt, for you will understand that, as the years had passed, and so many had not returned, the adventure had taken a very sinister tone, and, besides that, with the change of time, its legend becomes dimmer and less believed.

"But we said that, treasure or none, we would explore a country that had been hidden too long behind its barriers of forest and swamp. We started well equipped, as I have said, and all went well for the first week, during which we made good progress in our canoes, for so far (and, indeed, for a much longer time) the way is by water rather than land.

"But one night we landed, as the custom was, and slung our hammocks among the trees (for there was no dry ground at that place, and that time of year, and if there had been, no man would choose it for a couch, unless he would be eaten alive by ants, and other insects he could not name), and, in the morning we found that

20

one of the canoes had broken loose during the night, and floated away.

"It held stores that we were not willing to lose, so some of us— four in all—took a light canoe, and paddled down stream at a good pace to find it, and bring it back.

"We could not tell how long we should be likely to be, as we did not know at what hour it had broken loose, nor if it might blunder among the trunks of the flooded trees or be swept to the middle stream, so we had paddled hard, keeping a good look-out, and after about an hour we saw it grounded on a muddy shallow, with dryer ground at one side, as it seemed, but that was no more than a likely guess, the forest growing so dense to the water's edge.

"Well, we found that it had settled in the mud, so that it was not easy to move. We fastened it by a rope to our canoe, and two of us paddled to pull it off, and two others, of whom I was one, got out to push it along.

"Up to then we had not set eyes on an Indian, nor any sign of human life since we had left the settlements of civilisation behind. We seemed to have come to a vacant land. But suddenly we were surrounded by savages who rushed out from the trees.

"They had redwood swords, and had they sought our deaths we should have had a poor chance of escape—we two that were wading at least—but they had a different purpose in what they did.

"They were of a tribe that hunts men that they may be sacrificed in ceremonial ways, for which purpose they must be captured alive. Their method is to thrust at the thighs, so that they may secure their victims without inflicting a mortal wound, and as we knew what they would attempt when we saw the swords, we were able to hold them off for a time, defending ourselves with paddles which we snatched out of the canoe, and in the next minute our comrades opened fire, for there were two loaded rifles with them.... They shot straight, and one of the Indians fell, on which the others ran back into the trees, and the fight was done.

"But by that time I had taken a wound that had brought me down. It was the best I could do to fall into the boat, and when my companions, who stood by me stoutly enough, had got it afloat, and paddled back to where the others were waiting for our return, it was plain that I should be of no more use for that expedition.

"Well, I am making too long a tale of that which can be little to you, but was much to me at the time. What was to be done? If they took me on, it could only be to leave me when, at a later stage, they would have to abandon the boats, by which time it was certain that I should be unable to walk. If they left me there, it would be certain that I should be the Indians' meat, after being put to death with ceremonies I should be sure to dislike.

"I saw my companions look at each other and look at me, and I read that in their eyes which they would not say. I thought: 'If I go to sleep, or even if I am careless to turn my head, they will kill me, saying to themselves that it is the most merciful way, lest fall into the Indians' hands.'

"It was a thought which made my brain stir, though I was weak from the blood I lost, and I can remember now how the wound had commenced to burn and throb in a way that made thinking hard.

"I said: 'Give me the smallest canoe, which you can best spare, and food enough for a few days, and push me off to the middle stream, and I may come to Essabo alive. I shall go down in less time than we have taken against the strength of the stream. And I can paddle: my arms are sound.'

"Well, they were quick to agree. I knew they thought I had little chance, or I might say none, and few would few would say they were wrong; but it was a way out they were glad to take. I need not tell you I lived…. I suppose they were sorry for me, feeling whole themselves, and confident in the strength that their numbers gave, but they were never heard of again. They must have gone to their deaths, as eight hundred, first and last, at the best count I can make, had gone the same way before."

"It certainly," Devereux replied, "isn't a very promising enterprise for a stranger to undertake, even though the map may be good, for which there seems to be little proof. Fonseca must have judged me a fool if he thought that I would attempt it alone."

"Perhaps so. But you English have a reputation for such follies, so that it becomes an imputation you cannot avoid, especially when you are young and wander alone, and if you are staying in Manaos more than a day, I should advise you to let it be known that you are interested in Peixoto's map, for you will be safer if it is supposed that you have swallowed the bait."

"In that case, it will be well for you to tell me all that is known or which has grown with the years from the tale that Peixoto told, so that I may talk of it in a sensible way."

"So I will; though I have warned you to doubt how much may be true, or how much of it he ever said, for it is a most wonderful tale. And you will observe that, whether true or false, it has not proved of any use for the protection of those it should guide or warn. So, if I tell it, I must rely on you to take it for no more than it is. And, indeed, if I thought there were any fear that you might start on so vain a chase, I should give you an opposite warning from what I do. For it would be safer to let Fonseca have no knowledge of what you planned.

"You should know that he is said to traffic in secret drugs for which high prices are paid in London and the great cities of other lands. Cocaine is not the only strange drug that the Indians know. Fonseca traffics with them both up the river and here, and if he should pass the word to them that you are a spy upon what they sell, I do not suppose you would go even so far as a white man new to the land might be expected to do."

Señor Amerigo went on to tell a wild tale till the night was late, which it would be foolish to set down here, for so far as it was false (which it largely was, being verbal tradition which alters form as it passes from lip to lip) it would mislead, and so far as it was true, it would only be telling a tale which must be told for a second time, which it is well to avoid.

Also, there were matters in it to which Señor Amerigo himself could give no meaning, such as the warning which Hermes Peixoto was said to have been earnest to urge. "Do not drink it," he had declared, "do not drink the water, even though you see others do. For if you give way you will die."

"The difficulty in that," Amerigo said, "is that the water everywhere in the Amazon basin is wholesome to drink, and its quantity never fails. You could fill your own cup from the floods, so that you would have no fear of poison at all. And if you should see others drink, how could it be unwholesome to you?"

Chapter Three

Into the Unknown Land

DEVEREUX waked next morning with a revulsion of mood from that of the night before. He remembered that he had returned late, with confused, excited thoughts of an adventure to undertake, such as he had not supposed that the earth could give now that it was all measured and mapped, as he had thought it to be. His mind had fastened upon the fact that Peixoto had come back alive, even though he had come back to die. Might not another come back in a better way?

His experience must, at least, have been different from that of those who had not returned. Might not that difference have its root in the fact that he had gone alone? That there might be a better hope for a single man?

And Peixoto had not come with empty hands, and no more than a proofless tale. He had brought rich jewels, and they had not been in the rough. They had been cut and polished (he had asked Señor Amerigo that, and he had been explicit in his reply). That proved some part of the tale, though much less than all. Thinking thus, he had resolved that he would slip quietly away. Surely a single man could traverse the river courses, silently, unobserved, perhaps moving only during the night, with a better chance of passing peaceably through than if men should go in a company with a noise of guns to alarm the savages, to whom the great woods were a threatened home, and whose poisoned arrows would be deadly from the dense ambush from which they would be likely to come?

So he had dreamed, as he had walked back to the hotel through the moonlit streets, but the morning brought saner thoughts. Was it likely that he, a stranger, ignorant not merely of the impenetrable

24

forest of which Señor Amerigo had told, but of a hundred other things of which it would be needful to know, and which would be familiar to those who were native here—that he should succeed where all had failed for three hundred years? He put the thought from his mind. If he were to recover a shaken honour, and the fortune he once had had, he must use wits and money in more sensible ways.

Yet, having so resolved, his mind dwelt upon the idea with greater ease than before. Men may find it pleasure to dream of that which would be folly to plan. And while he dreamed he was impelled toward the attempt by a fact which he did not consciously weigh. He was like a man who cannot remain where he is, and who is made aware of an open gate where all others are shut to him. He may like or fear the road that it shows, but in the end he will go through.

The fact was that his partner's defalcations and flight, the news of which had reached him almost as he had landed at Rio, had not only swept away the bulk of the small fortune his father left: they had cast a shadow upon himself from under which it was not easy to move.

He knew that his visit to Rio—on business which his partner had proposed, and which had proved on arrival to be of a very visionary kind—gave him the appearance of having absconded from trouble about to come. To return to England would be to face the certain indignity of arrest, and a possible conviction for frauds which were not his. Even here, he did not know but that he might be reached by the patient implacable obstinacy of English law.

And it was for business in this country that he had been trained: it was its language that he had learned. If he would wander further away, where should he go except to the great wilderness which stretched around and ahead?

In the next weeks he found Señor Amerigo a friend with whom it had become pleasant to sit, and though he would dissuade him from serious thoughts of Peixoto's goal, and it was agreed that they talked in no more than an idle way, yet the idea was a subject of frequent debate, and he learnt much which, if he should venture so wild a quest, it would be needful to know.

There was a day when he sat under the vines of Señor Amerigo's patio, and said: "You will think me, mad, but I have decided to go. There is a cargo-boat in from Bristol on which I saw a light skiff, which, as I said to the captain, could not be very useful to him being unfit for the sea.

"Well, in a word, he agreed the price, and the boat is mine."

"On our rivers," Señor Amerigo replied doubtfully, "men prefer the paddle and the canoe."

"So they may, but I am more used to a boat. As a fact I can row better than most. I was stroke of a college crew."

Señor Amerigo looked at him in a moment's silence. He was aware of a purpose he could not change. He said no more than: "If you are resolved, I will wish you well."

Four days later, a river steamer, plying up to Essabo with many calls at the settlements which are to be found on the river banks, took the skiff on board, with the stores that Devereux had been counselled to buy, and the first stage of one of the wildest adventures on which even a wandering Briton ever staked his life had begun.

The little steamer, taking in wood for fuel from time to time at the quays where it tied up, went on day by day up a river that gradually narrowed till both banks could be clearly seen, and after that along a branch stream to the south, where there were still occasional clearings and human life on its wooded banks.

But these clearings, even from when Manaos had been left behind, had been no more than narrow, precarious footholds between the flood before and the crowding forest behind. For from the dense forest there came a pressure hat never ceased, either night or day, to snatch back the little patches of tillage that had been cleared by the petty efforts of human hands, and reassert its sovereignty of the land. It seemed to be ever pushing them back with contemptuous strength to the river from which they came.

And behind was the green, unchanging twilight of fronds that no winter found, of boughs that were never bare. A forest so dense of growth that to be five yards apart might be much the same as to be five miles away. A forest festooned and choked with lianas and clinging vines, so that, while it would be hard for any creature to move below, except where the waterways made clear shadowed aisles under closing boughs, life of jaguar and monkey, of snake and sloth, moved freely beneath the green roof of the twilight world, with no fear of falling to the far ground below, as in fact, it would not have been easy to do.

THE SCREAMING LAKE, BY S. FOWLER WRIGHT

Devereux looked at this living wall from the steamer's deck as it went on for its endless leagues, and if his heart sank somewhat, it was a feeling he would not own. He looked at it, after that, from the lower view of a skiff's thwart, but it was then mostly by moonlight, or light of stars, for he rowed, as he had purposed, during the night, keeping the middle stream; and when daylight came he would draw in to the, bank, and tie up where he would be covered by friendly boughs, in which he would swing his hammock, and hope that he would not be drenched before night returned by a deluge of tropic rain.

He went on long in this way, forgetting the count of days, till the river narrowed, and became a network of channels of which the right one would not always be easy to choose, and now he found that he must make more use of the day, and even so there would be place where there would be little light, in passages narrow to thread.

It was after he had struck a blunt-nosed saurian with the boat's bow, startling both parties concerned, but with no more trouble than that, that he decided that he must abandon the sculls.

He had brought one of the round-bladed paddles that are preferred by the boatmen of the lower Amazon, and now he crouched in the bow, striking the water left and right, and seeing the way he went, which it was prudent to do where tree-roots would often spread out in the narrow stream.

Now the sunlight would only penetrate through the meeting boughs, if at all, at the height of noon. The forest bushes might be brilliant with flowers, the colours of a thousand various wings, from the humming-birds to the crowds of quarrelling parroquets and the bright macaws, might flash dazzlingly where the sunlight struck, but otherwise they would be tamed by the blue-green shadows that were their natural home. The raucous cries of the birds, fitted to penetrate through the heavy leaves and the steaming air, were a discord that seldom died, as was the noise of the screaming, chattering monkeys that made their homes in the boughs above. But the weeks went, with no sound of a human voice, no sight of a human form....

Overhead, in the intervals of the rain, there must have been open blue, and there was doubtless power in the blaze of the midday sun, but that was far off, where the forest, reaching upward, fought for the light. Below, there was no excess of heat for a tropic land, but there was moisture everywhere from which there was no escape; and when the rain came, streaming down through whatever thickness of leafy boughs, and saturating the choked undergrowth, and the lianas that festooned the intervals of the crowding trees, it was impossible to do anything but find such shelter as the moment allowed, and crouch in the cover that oilskin gave.

For he found that he had come to an amphibious land. There was water—warm water not only beneath the boat and between the trees, but in the air, and soaking through from above, with a hot evaporation that never ceased. The dawn after the rain would be blind with mist. The evening would be mist-hidden again, after the deluge that fell in the afternoon. But the heat, enervating by moisture though it might be, was not over great under the green gloom of the trees. He could paddle hard enough while the rain held off, and he found channels which, though they twisted about, would still take him, more or less, in the direction he sought.

He had learned that the tropic night is alive, and the dawn is loud, but he had thought that the afternoon was still, until he became aware that he must have been partly wrong about that when an absolute silence came, such as he had not noticed before. It was as though the forest had ceased to breathe and crouched motionless in a waiting fear. And after the silence a darkness fell, so that he had a moment's wonder of whether he might not have mistaken the length of the monotonous day.

The air became hot and still, and the high dim isles of the water-courses mysterious, sinister, indistinct in the black gloom, which gave them a vague immensity beyond even that which they would show to the light of the tropic moon.

He knew that there must be something approaching now beyond the ordinary downpour of the afternoon, and became instinctively one with the fear that the forest felt. He drew the boat to the side of a rising bank, and moored it under the rankest growth that spread outward above the stream.

Far above, where there had been a sunlit surface a green that had been dried by the midday heat, the clouded heaven had come down like a brooding bird to the height that the forest rose.

It covered the trees with a soft grey breast that bore the rain which was ever craved by that sunburned surface of vivid green and brilliant exotic flowers, but it was a breast in which lightnings bred. The green ocean-surface, which had no part in the sombre darkness below, stirred with a fearful delight of the coming rain. Its upper boughs, from which the chattering monkeys had fled, murmured and

28

moved. They lifted to feel the cool caress of the settling cloud, which burst at last in such a deluge of threshing rain as taught them how weak they were.

There was no wind, but the downpour flattened the boughs, so that the wide ocean of leaves was crushed like a trodden field. Its whole surface sank under the sudden weight of the rain. And with the rain there had come a thunder that did not cease, and a lightning that stabbed ever downward among the trees. It lit the dense gloom below with a ghostly, flickering, but continuous light, as it bored its black shafts of death, narrow and deep, that drove down to the distant ground.

Tomorrow, the forest would care little for that, having become active to heal its wounds. The surrounding life would crowd swiftly into those funnels of death, mounting on shrivelled vines, and eating into the dead tree-trunks that the rain would rot in the coming week. In a month there would not be so much as a hidden scar where there had come death to a forest lord, and to monkey and bird and a million insects that had sheltered throughout its depths.

CHAPTER FOUR

THE FIRST CHECK

THE rain penetrated the two hundred feet of tangle of vine and bough, not in drops, which it was too dense to permit, but in spouts of water that forced apertures through leaf and branch, and poured downward as though a million cisterns had leaked above. They struck on the surface of the stream, and on the broad leaves of the water-plants with a force that cast them upward again in cascades of spray. The atmosphere became water rather than air, and when a time came that the thunder died, and the lightning ceased, the gloom of the under-world was made worse than before by a mist that steamed upward from every leaf, until this was turned to a multicolour of light, as a ray of the sun that was now regnant again in the unseen blue struck down through the narrow aisle of the watercourse, and made the mist a flashing dazzle of rainbow light, like a dewdrop of monstrous size.

Devereux watched, and was wet. He knew from what he had learned of lesser deluges in the last weeks, that the oilskin cover that he had stretched over the boat, stout though it was, would have been insufficient to protect its contents. It was, indeed, an atmosphere where nothing was ever dry, for the moisture was not merely upon the ground. It did not only fall from the sky. It was in the drenched air, which was wet to breathe. It penetrated everywhere but into the sealed cans, in which his food was stored, and whatever else must be kept dry for its use to last.

His clothing had become less and less in these days, until now it was next to none. He had found the truth of a warning that Señor Amerigo had given when he had seen that he was determined to come: "You may wear clothes if you choose when you are in the land of the forest rains, but they will always be wet, and the more you wear, the more you will be likely to die."

Now he looked out on a jewelled gloom in which life resumed, brilliant in colour, and discordant in raucous cries. High overhead, the long-tailed monkeys whistled and screamed, and the parrots called, discussing, and doubtless cursing the storm. Butterflies, topaz and green, sulphur and flaming scarlet, fluttered out from the under sides of the dripping leaves. Even a jaguar's cry in the distant trees had a joyous sound, and did nothing to still the impatient life that the lightnings had not consumed. Red dragonflies flashed through the gleaming mist that was no brighter than they. At three yards' distance, a half-grown boa glided into the water in a straight, purposeful way, and swam out with easy sinuous movements, its head showing for a moment, and then being hidden by the pervading mist. It took no notice of Devereux, at which he was unsurprised, having learnt already that if he avoided sudden movements or sounds, and went quietly his separate way, the teeming forest life would take as little notice of him, either to advance in anger or shrink in fear, or even to pause from pursuit of its own affairs.

And through the steam of the rain-drenched air, the scent of decay that rose ever from the rot of the fecund ground had become so constant that he had ceased to notice its pervading presence, now called with recruited strength, compelling consciousness of its message of the death that all life requires.

There would still be some hours of day before the quick twilight fell, and he hesitated as to whether he should attempt a further advance, or be content with the progress already made. Indecision ceased when he observed a convenient branch where he could swing his hammock clear of surrounding leaves, which had not always been easy to find. So he had a meal in the best comfort he could contrive, eating without stint, as he might do while he could stay with the boat, which still held far more than he would try to load on his own back, slung the hammock, and was quickly asleep in a world which he had found (except some insects) willing to leave him alone while he would treat it in the same way, and which he believed to be empty of men.

He waked to the coming dawn, which was proclaimed by a thousand voices before the dim light had pierced downward to where he lay. He rose quickly, having formed a habit of using the whole of the morning hours while the heat was least, and looked down on steaming mud, where there had been water the night before.

At a short distance away, the moored boat lay half in water and half aground, and it was clear that, if the water were still receding, he had no moment to lose if he were to get it afloat, and clear of the shallow in which it lay.

It was a danger on which Señor Amerigo had not been silent, but it was not one which he had been able to tell him how to avoid. As the great branches of the water system of the Amazon valley are left behind, and the traveller penetrates deeper inland among the streams and swamps from which they are fed, or which their surplus waters provide, there is a constant, ever-increasing danger that a recession of water will leave him aground in a position from which his craft may be floated again in a few hours, or may remain, in the absence of portage (which may be for ten yards or as many miles), for a whole season before the steaming, pool-broken mud becomes a course of running water again.

Devereux knew that, soon or late, he must abandon the boat, and depend for safety and sustenance on no more than he could bear on his own back through the steaming heat, as he must struggle on through the choked growth of the pathless way; and he was too vague as to the distance to be traversed, or that which he had already come, to guess how soon this would be. But he had not expected it to be yet. Not for weeks to come.

He knew, if Peixoto's tale or his map were true, that he would come clear at last from the forest plain to a sight of hills in a region of open land. Till that time, he had only to keep as straight a course as natural obstacles would permit, with his compass for guide. But how much of the forest would still remain to be crossed when he would abandon the boat was an unguessable chance, on which success or failure might largely hang. But he was sure that this was soon—a month too soon, if not more.

Sinking almost knee-deep in the soft, warm, treacherous mud, and indifferent in this instant peril to the living dangers about his feet, he heaved at the boat's stern until he had the satisfaction of feeling that it slid forward on to a floating keel. But the moment was short. He was scarcely aboard before it grounded again.

Releasing it once more, and in shorter time, he paddled for some minutes along an alley of water that was shallow, but did not fail. Then he came to a deeper channel, but one that too him almost directly backward from the direction he wished to take.

The morning hours were spent in a baffled effort to find some passage deep enough for the boat, and which did not lead away from the course he sought. At the end of that time, he reckoned that he must have lost several miles, and was no nearer to finding a forward channel.

He was exasperated at this time to see deep water on his left hand, almost within reach, but separated by a muddy, tree-cumbered shallow, which broadened and rose until the further water was hidden from view. When he caught it again, it gleamed through an aisle of shade, showing by that that it was broad enough for the sun to reach downward between branches that did not meet. As he went on paddling in the opposite direction from that which he wished to take, he began to debate in his mind whether it would not have been better to attempt to get the boat across to that deeper water, even though it should have meant unloading all its contents. He thought that he had seen no obstacle over which he might not have dragged the empty boat.

But it was not a thing to turn back to attempt, unless the advantage were sure. What was the extent and direction of that water which had been near and had looked wide? He determined to tie up the boat and make a short exploration under the trees, which did not appear at this point to be set very closely together, nor was the sodden ground at their roots cumbered with undergrowth too dense to be broken through.

He had largely lost his fear of the forest at this time. He had grown familiar with it from the comparative security of the boat. Even the dreaded mosquitoes had not troubled him after the first few days, for they are a plague from which the Amazon basin is, in some places, capriciously free. And as to men, there had been no sign in all these weeks that there had been any there from the dawn of time.

But he drew on wading-boots that were strong and high, and put on a coat, less as a protection from the pricks he was sure to meet than for the convenience its pockets gave. He did not think it necessary to cumber himself with the rifle, which he had ceased to draw from its waterproof case, but he put a revolver in his pocket, less from any expectation that it would be of use than from recognition of the etiquette the occasion required. He took a machete in a more practical mood, and set out on what he did not intend to be more than a short survey.

So it was. Probably shorter than he had meant, if maximum distance from the boat be the standard by which to judge. When he got safely back, two or three hours later, under a deluge of rain, he may not have been more than three hundred yards distant at any time. He had done little, and seen less, but he had learnt more.

For one thing, he had experienced the terror that comes to those who are lost in that illimitable wilderness without hope of escape. He had experienced solitude he had not known it before.

It had happened, as it seemed, at a step. He had been making what he thought to be a straight confident way, slowly indeed, but surely enough, when he had stumbled in a ground-vine tangle, and broken free to become aware that the forest growth was a wall around him on every side, and that direction was lost.

He thought at first that it was a matter of a step or two, with a few good machete blows that would bring him clear, but he found he was wrong in that. He hacked and struggled on for the next hour in a growing fear. He could not tell in the least whether he were getting nearer to the boat or further away. He might observe that he was on a higher level than that to which the water had risen in recent weeks, by the growth that the ground had borne, but how much meaning was there in that? He could wish that he had brought a compass for guide, as he surely ought to have done, but there was no avail in regret.

He knew that, if he were lost, his position would be worse—far worse—than if he had been obliged to abandon the boat in a deliberate way, for now he was without a score of essential things on which life must rely. He was without the rifle on which food and defence might entirely depend. He had not the hammock, light to carry, but able to give him sleep clear of the night-damp, insect-infested ground. He had not—but what use was there in thinking thus? He must get back to the boat, or he would be no better than dead.... Overhead, a jaguar barked in the trees.

He looked up at the sound, and his movement drew the eyes of the beast, which had not observed him before. Its teeth showed in a snarl blended of ferocity and surprise, and perhaps fear. He had the sense and nerve to remain silent and still, and after a moment of hesitation it gave a lithe swift spring, which hid it among the leaves.

He had a new fear after that, lest at any moment he might feel its paws on his back, and its hot fanged mouth reaching round for his throat, that would be so easy to tear, but even for that he could not lose the more urgent imminent dread that he would not get back to the boat.

Desperation improved his wit. It was plainly dangerous to continue in a direction that might be taking him further away. But if he should retreat his course, which should be simple to do through the hacked and trampled vines, he could start in another direction from the spot where he had first been conscious that he was lost. If he should continue to make short excursions from there until he should find the path which he had cut, no forest could be so dense that it would not yield its secret at last, where the area of necessary exploration must be so small.

This he did, having shock enough when he found how far from straight, and how few yards was the way he had come, but by persistence in the plan he had formed, he came free at last, and back to the boat, which had the look of a lost home, just as the afternoon rain became heavy among the trees.

CHAPTER FIVE

ON THE ROOF OF THE FOREST WORLD

THE experience through which he had passed, short though it was, had been sufficient to strengthen his resolution not to abandon the boat, while it also disinclined him from further risks of the same kind. He was tired by the exertions that he had made, and as the night was not far off he resolved to remain where he was till the next day, but he first took the precaution of marking the water-level, and looking at it again in an hour's time, when it appeared that it was unchanged, so that he should not fear to wake again to the sight of a stranded boat.

As he lay awake in his hammock that night, he looked up at the dense concourse of trees, standing blackly in the clear uncoloured light of the tropic moon, and an idea came. Why should he not climb to the roof of that forest world, and see whether there were any sign of water around, or perhaps that he were nearer its limit than he had guessed? It would be no harm at the worst, and it should be quite easy to do.

So when morning came he looked for a tree that was straight and high, but not bare of lateral boughs, as those of the palm varieties were, and he climbed with ease. Indeed, as he moved upward through the dim green world that was as remote from the sun above us as from the fecund rot of the swamp below, he saw that it would be hard to find a place for unhindered fall.

But he found that he was no longer unconsidered or unobserved. The tree-dwellers were alert to the danger of large creatures that came up from the ground. The parrots fled with a squawking of many throats that alarmed a hundred birds of as brilliant hues though less voluble tongues. The spider-monkeys dodged around, curious

36

but wary, with warning whistles to their companions of where he came. They were not far away, but in constant movement among the trees, and he saw that it would have required a good aim, at an instant's uncertain sight, to bring them down, either with a bullet, or the short straight flight of a blowpipe's dart.

He climbed on in a growing light, which he did not like. He blinked blindly against the sun. He had become used, for so many weeks, to the half-light of the shaded streams, and to look right and left into the deeper gloom of the forest depths, that his eyes had become unequal to face the glare of the tropic sun. Turning his back to the east, where it was still low, he waited awhile, looking down, and then shading his eyes, as they became more equal to face the light. He was able to look round after a time, but what was there to see?

Beauty enough, for one of a leisured mood. A dark-green ocean of varnished leaves that swayed in the morning wind, and here and there an eruption of splendid flower. His trouble was that he could see but a short way. He was like a fish that comes up from the ocean depths. It may see the sky and the nearer waves, but how far can it look round, beyond them? Not at all.

The tree he had climbed did not rise above its fellows, which it would not have been easy for it to do. The forest surface was flatter than the waves of a windy sea. Standing on the topmost bough that would bear his weight, he could see for twenty yards, here and there, with further glimpses as the giant palm-fronds around him swayed in the wind. He saw that he had made a wise choice in the tree he climbed, for the most of the trees were tufted high above the trunk, where a climb must end. The trouble was that the whole forest had the same will for the sun. The trees must reach up to an equal height, unless they had been thwarted and choked in the damp heat of the fierce conflict below.

Here it was not damp. It was dry and hot. The great trees drew one strength from the sun, and another from the dark swamps that were far below which the sun could not reach to dry. Those were the conditions of life, for which they fought with ruthless relentless wills, and for which the creeping vines clutched each other and them, and climbed up with a strangling hold.

It appeared to Devereux that when he thought he could see far by that climb he had made a bad guess. Yet he was not one to be easily foiled. Once, in the course of a swaying gust, he thought that he saw a place where the surface of the green ocean rose. He waited patiently till the wind came with the same caprice, and this time he was sure.

He decided to reach that spot, which should not be hard, and was then deterred by a memory of yesterday's fear. He would not risk being lost again for much more than he would be likely to see.

But he considered that there was no possible doubt of that, if he were cautious in what he did. Here he had the sun's help. He could observe that the loftier trees he sought were almost due south of his own position. If he were careful to make his return due north, he could not be far away from the tree by which he had climbed, and to find it could only be a matter of time. The clump of loftier trees would be a mark that he could not miss, and to which he could return, if need be, a dozen times. In such a case he could not become utterly lost. The chances were large that he would not be lost at all.

The tree by which he had climbed was not of a common kind. It had rather large elongated leaves, dark green, streaked with grey. It was a kind of leaf more common among the low growths of the swamps than the major trees. He broke its topmost branch, so that he could identify it beyond doubt, and began to make way through the trees, keeping sufficiently near the surface to watch the sun, so that he should not swerve from a straight course. So he came to the place he sought, where the forest roof was lifted by a rise of the ground below.

Here he got a further sight, being able to mount perhaps thirty feet above the level of the green ocean that stretched away westward, and seemed to have no limit at all. That was the limit of what he learned: that the forest had no limit that could be seen in the clear air, no break in the swaying dark-green carpet of frond and bough. It was not much to learn, for he knew he could not see very far at that height. He half-circled the group of the loftier trees, but got no more than the same vision of swaying green, over which a great hawk moved on slow broad wings, waiting to stoop, as fishing-eagles move over the sea.

So far, he had gained little to pay his pains. He knew only that there was no stretch of water within some miles that was broad enough to prevent the green ocean having an unbroken aspect from the little height he had gained, and he might have guessed that, and spared the loss of the finest part of the day. He became in haste to get back, and conscious of aching unaccustomed muscles that would be glad to rest again on a boat's thwart.

He did not work round the circle of the higher trees on his return, having no more expectation of anything it would be advantage to see. He went straight ahead, through the midst of the boughs, and so came to something he had not sought, and would have chosen to miss.

CHAPTER SIX

A BIRD'S-EYE VIEW

DEVEREUX came to a place where he could go straight forward no more, for the trees stopped. He looked down on a circular clearing, in the midst of which there was a single conical hut of a great size. It was steeply built, so that from above it looked to be narrower than it was. He saw small patches of tilled ground. He saw figures move. He knew he had come to one of the Indian dwellings of which he had been told, and he became as still as the branch he held.

It seemed to him a strange chance that he should thus have come upon one of their communal dwellings, such as he could not doubt it to be, and which are said to be so well hidden in woods so dense that even their nearest neighbours do not know where they are, after he had travelled so long without seeing a living man. But the explanation was simple enough. He had been drawn to that spot by the greater height of the trees, and the Indians had chosen the spot from the same cause—that it was a higher place, to which the floods would be unlikely to rise.

Here, on the forest roof, the difference in height made it a conspicuous place, but that would not be observable from below. In fact, the settlement had covered most of the rising ground, so that the higher trees, around which he had come at first, were a mere fringe for this open circular space, into which he looked down as one might view a bear pit of a great size.

He thought the shape of the narrow conical hut to be foolishly queer, but there was reason for that. It rose high to defeat the floods, which would rise at times to a level that made a wooded lake of the whole land: its sides were steep to present the least resistance to the frequent tempestuous rain that descended upon it.

The house was not built for warmth, for here there was no cold in the night, nor any winter season at all. It was built to defeat water alone, for which it could not have been better shaped.

Devereux watched those who had no suspicion of him. He saw men go into the forest, and others return. He saw women work on the crops. There were some young children that ran about. The men wore loin cloths, supported by belts in which hung weapons or tools. The women and children wore precisely nothing, unless it were a necklace of caiman's teeth, or a jaguar's claw.

To Devereux, looking down on their olive-brow bodies, they appeared to be vigorous, well-made healthy, more alert than he had observed the civilised men of this tropic land to be. So they were. They maintained a high standard of health, among other ways, by holding their new-born babies under water a sufficient time to make sure that the weaklings died.

If a baby were ill-formed, or unpleasing in any way, its mother could be relied upon to hold it under long enough to make doubly sure, so that she would not need to produce it for the derision of other eyes, for parturition was a lonely affair.

Devereux could see their forms, which he was bound to approve. He could not see their faces so well, which he might have liked less.

He saw that they all, children, women and men, lived nakedly in a single abode, and he thought by that that they must be savages of a low kind. So, in some ways, they were. But in this matter he was largely misled by analogies which did not apply. The dwellings sheltered them from the rain while they slept, and preserved their tools, which were the main uses it had. Within its bounds they were held by an etiquette which had the force of the strictest law. No man within that conical wall would so much as touch his own wife with a kindly hand. Their privacies were for the forest depths. It was the home that was public here.

There were good reasons for this, as for the fact that they went unclad, but because they might be condemned on a wrong count it did not follow that they were less than base. They were human, compounded of bad and good, and their eyes, which were cruel and small, held no mercy for any stranger about their gates.

Devereux watched them for a time going in and out, and about their daily affairs. He was sure that he would not be observed while he remained still. He was less sure how it would be when he should move, as at last he must.

But he had no mind to remain till dark, and attempt return in the night. He was stiff and tired. Sooner or later, he must withdraw as quietly as he could contrive.

He saw men go, mostly with hunting weapons, or come back with the spoils they won. He noticed that they took no regular paths, but pushed out through the undergrowth anywhere, which, being so treated, in that fecund wet heated soil, would doubtless heal any wounds of passage they made in a space of hours, so that it would soon become invisible to the keenest eyes.

But he noticed that there was one side upon which none went out or in, and he determined that that should be the one by which he would attempt to get back to the boat. He had been observant upon what was a deliberate fact, but the deduction he made was wrong. They avoided that side because it was there that their treasure lay, being the unmarried girls of the tribe. So it came that it was not long before he was looking down on a smaller hut, though of the same shape. The cleared space was smaller also, but it was enough for the seven girls he saw, who were learning a dance that a woman taught.

CHAPTER SEVEN

DUEL AMONG THE TREES

THE practice of segregating unmarried girls, which has become general among the Amazonian Indians over enormous territories into which civilised men rarely or never penetrate, is of comparatively recent origin, appears to have no relation to their own sexual customs, and may be the sole instance in which the impact of European civilisation has disturbed the established traditions by which they live.

By ancient, reasonable custom, a captured enemy should be killed, as prudence dictates (should we let him loose to use his blowpipe on our own backs, or to steal the turtles' eggs from our own stream?); and he may also be eaten, or at least his best joints, for it will be a particular insult to him, and what merit can there be in the waste of excellent food? (But we do not eat the kidneys nor other offensive internal organs either of men or any other creatures, as the white savages are said to do. we are cleanly men!) Pitiless strife there had always been under pressure of economic laws which made human existence hard; but the taking of slaves with the possible exception of very young children, was unknown till the white men came.

Even the capture of wives, though it might be simulated in bridal ceremonies, had become extinct, if it had ever prevailed; for what use would there be in capturing a woman whom there would be no means to detain? And one who (which would be much worse than her loss) might betray the position of the lodge to which she had been brought.

But in the last centuries there had come change. There had risen a market for slaves in the white settlements along the river banks and the distant coast. It was for slaves of various kinds, often masquerading in other names, as religion or law required, but constant in its demand for young unmarried Indian girls.

The far depths of the forest might be secure from the white men's raids, but not from that of the next Indian tribe, and girls once caught could be bartered from lodge to lodge, till they would come at the far last to the estate of some wealthy *estanciero*, who would purchase them for his own use, or a river-captain who would take them down to the great city beside the sea.

In either case, a girl so bartered would have no hope of escape. It would be impossible, almost from the day when she was seized, for her to find her way back to the remote and nameless spot in the million miles of the forest from which she had been hurried away, and which, till then, she may never have left for as much as five hundred yards of its changeless gloom. They would accept fate, perhaps not always with hardship or much regret, and became the mothers of the half-breed *mestizos* who are now so large a proportion of the inhabitants of the civilised provinces of Brazil.

The Indian tribes, finding existence threatened by pillage of those from whom the next generation should come, had replied with this protective device. Their communal lodges, hidden in the deepest glooms of the pathless forest, might not be easy to find. But they must be daily going out and in, and might be tracked or watched in spite of all their precautions, and the remorseless slaughter of alien spies. So they would make a separate and yet deeper seclusion only and very circumspectly to be approached by those who took it the food required, apart from which none went out or in, and here, from an early age, they shut the unmarried girls until puberty (which would come late in that sunless gloom) should fit them for marriage and the motherhood that the tribe required....

Devereux looked down on six bodies of olive-brown and one that was of a lighter hue. He saw six that were comely enough, though with a tendency to be thick and short. He saw one that was taller and more slender, so that the difference of height appeared to more than it was. He was not unwilling to look, but he was most unwilling to be looked at. For the moment, he remained absolutely still. While he remained so, he looked down, which was a sufficient reason that he did not see a man who was in the tree-tops on the opposite side, and who was even stiller than he.

The man, who was stationed there to see that no harm approached to the virgins' lodge without alarm, which it would be his duty to raise, looked at Devereux in a natural wonder of what he was. He knew the appearance of the Indians of his own, and of all the neighbouring tribes, but this was something he had not met. He knew only that it was a stranger he saw and he had been born to the knowledge that a stranger is not a friend.

His glance searched the trees, but could observe no evidence that Devereux was not alone. If he had no support, it appeared to show that he had come not to attack but to spy. The first necessity, in that case, was not to raise alarm, but to make sure that the spy did not escape. Very cautiously, he shifted his position somewhat among the leaves, to give him a clearer sight, and put a well-poisoned arrow to the string of his bow.

Devereux had his feet on one branch, and his hand on another that crossed before him, over which he leaned to look down. He was aware that this branch quivered, as though it had been struck a sharp blow. He looked at an arrow-shaft that had not been there a moment before. He touched it with a startled hand, and it broke off at the point to which it had entered the tree. He saw with a half conscious surprise that it had been cut almost completely through at the point at which it had broken off. He remembered, in the back of his mind, that he had been told of this Indian custom the purpose of which was that it should be more difficult to draw the poisoned point from the wound.

The thought did not delay his eyes, which were instant to look in the direction from which the arrow had come. He saw the Indian, who thought, with some excuse that the first arrow had found its mark, in the act of setting another to the cord, to make probability sure.

Devereux might have had time to withdraw from sight before the shaft flew, though it would have been a close doubt, but he tried a quicker and bolder course. He pulled out his revolver and fired. The shot missed, but may have disconcerted the Indian's aim, for the second shaft was less accurate than the first.

There followed a duel of shaft and shot, the issue of which might be hard to guess. The range was extreme for accuracy, either with revolver or bow. The Indian had the advantage of greater practice and skill, but he had the slower weapon, and a disadvantage of light, for while the forest-dwellers can see much better in the gloom to which they are born than any white men are likely to do, the sight of their small, deep-set eyes is worse in the full light of the sun, and the situation of the combatants was such that it was high overhead, but rather behind Devereux's back.

The revolver was emptied before the Indian had equalled the accuracy of his first attempt. Devereux, whose last two shots had been more deliberate than the earlier ones he had realised that haste and waste are as much alike as the words sound, was in the act of retreat, having no mind to remain a mark now that his weapon was empty, when he saw that his enemy was pitching forward, as one whose balance hard to keep. He saw him slip through a cracking of boughs for some thirty feet, fall outward, bounce on an out-jutting branch, and somersault to the distant ground.

Devereux's eyes followed his fall, and looked down on girls who no longer danced, and whose upturned faces had become easy to see. He saw seven (including that of the instructress) which were flat-featured, with high cheek-bones, and small recessed eyes, though these general characteristics were subject to much individual variation, and were even allied to some pulchritudes of youth and sex. He saw another face of a different kind.

But he had no leisure to look at bare bodies, nor faces evil or good, nor was he in any mood to admire, had they possessed the beauties of Grecian art. As a fact, he might have seen more had he not been two hundred feet overhead, where the light was more strong than below. But he had no trouble for that, having more urgent affairs.

He considered quickly that, if his assailant had been alone, he might be in no present peril, but that there would now be alarm was sure, and pursuit seemed an almost equal certainty. How quickly he could get back to the boat had become a question of life and death, and he began to push through the boughs, making the half-circuit of this open space which delayed his direct advance, and careless now of whether or not he might be visible to the women below.

CHAPTER EIGHT

DUEL PRELUDES DUET

HE who seeks to make speed through the forest roof must have eyes only for where he goes, however thick may be the eager branches that struggle upward to reach the light. Devereux saw no more of a sharp scuffle below, or of a hardwood dagger thrust through a woman's side by a strong young hand, than of the spider-monkeys that whistled mockery of his clumsy progress among the trees.

He had worked round the open space, and was, (he hoped) making a straight way to the tree by which he had climbed when he was aware of pursuit that came from below, following him faster than he could flee, while it was also gaining his height. It could not be far, in that thickness of leaves, or he would not have been aware of it at all. It must be coming straight on his track, guided, he supposed, by the noise he made, and making better progress than his, or the sounds would not be louder, nearer, than a moment before. Well, if he could not fly, he must try the only remedy that remained.

He paused in a tree's fork, breaking his revolver and reloading it with hasty fingers, and as he closed it again, with no second to lose, his pursuer appeared through the leaves.

"Why have you stopped?" a girl's voice asked sharply in Portuguese. "Don't you know which way to go?"

"I beg your pardon," he replied to the half-seen nudity that seemed so unconscious of itself, "you shouldn't have followed me like that. You very nearly got shot."

"What did you expect me to do when you didn't wait?"

"I didn't expect anything. How was I to know you were there?"

"How were you to know? Well, when you had got that far, and shot Teripa, you might have waited to see. After I'd had to knife the old witch, I could still see the way you were going off.... I suppose you'll say next you didn't see me do that?"

"I'm afraid not. I was too anxious to get away myself; and, besides, how could I have guessed that anyone would be there?"

As he spoke, he gave no attention to a bird's cry raucous, penetrating and shrill, which could be heard three times from the ground below, and was then thrice repeated from a distance away. But the girl knew it for the signal it was.

"Well," she said impatiently, "it's no use staying to talk. Don't wait for me. Get ahead. I can climb faster than you seem able to do." And then, with a sharper doubt, as the implications of his last words entered her mind: "I suppose you know where you're going? You're not lost, are you? *You're not alone?*"

"I'm alone, but I'm not lost. At least, I hope not. I've got a boat, if we can reach it before we're caught."

The girl stopped dead. She said no more to urge him to go on, nor gave any sign of following.

"*Alone?*" she repeated, in a voice in which terror and amazement strove. "You mean no one's with you at all? How do you hope we can get away?" And then, with intuitive realisation of what must have been incredibly unlikely to her: "You mean that we're both in the same mess? You didn't come to find me at all?"

"No," he said. "I've no idea who you are. But it's silly to lose time talking here. I've got a boat, and I've got to get to it, if it's not too late now.... You can go back, if you like. I should think it might be the best thing to do."

The girl appeared to hesitate, as though she were inclined to the same view. Then she said bitterly: "I can't do that now I've killed Chaota. What a mess you've got me into!"

"If we stay here, it'll be a bigger mess than it is now.... I hadn't asked you to come." He spoke with a bitterness equal to her own. He saw himself to be involved in a desperate position from which it seemed that, if he came clear, he was to have a young woman upon his hands who would almost certainly require him to turn back to the civilisation from which, by her speech, she had surely come. And a young woman of unpleasant temper, and many uncertainties of what she might prove to be. One who talked of *him* getting *her* into a

48

mess! Her own unreason must be excuse for the rudeness of his reply.

"I don't want to stay here," she answered, in a milder voice, "and it's silly to quarrel. We haven't time. But we can't go back to the ground now, looking for boats. Not till after dark. If they haven't found it by then, we can get away. They're never out after dark. They're afraid. They think the devil would get his own.... I can show you where they won't find us till then, if it's still to let."

She turned, as she spoke, and began to climb in another direction, looking back for him to follow, which he did reluctantly, neither liking the turn of events, nor sure that there was wisdom in the course which she had chosen for both.

It still seemed to him that the best chance of escape would be to get quickly to the boat. Surely, every moment of delay would increase the probability that it would be discovered, and the position rendered desperate by its loss, even though they might hide successfully for a time, or get away through the trees. But it was a case of one being of doubtful mind, and one sure, and the latter won, as must always be.

They went on for about half an hour, the girl leading in an assured way, which must pause for him at times, even though, as she went on, she descended half down through the trees to where there was a maximum density in the tangled twilight through which they must force a way, and they were divided equally from the ground, that was a hundred feet below, and the light that was the same distance above. As she led, she was hidden from a clear view by the thickness of leaves and the dim light, but she must stop at last, which she did in the fork of a giant trunk, so that he came to her side.

She was either become in fact as unconscious by habit of her own nudity, as were the Indian girls among whom she had been confined, or so, with a woman's simulation, which is always more than a man has at command, she would make it appear; and, indeed, the occasion was not one to encourage wandering or self-conscious thoughts in one who had seen how the Soquito Indians dealt with their captured foes. Devereux, with less exactness of knowledge to sharpen fear, was as aware as herself of the extremity of the peril from which they fled; and, beyond that, he had a feeling of exasperation at this caprice of unlikely fate, that might place him in a dilemma of conflict between chivalry and the attempt for which he had risked so much. So that it was with little consciousness of themselves, or of the conventions in which they had been equally bred, that they bent together to look down a narrow space that divided the trunk upon which they clung from that of another tree of almost an equal girth.

She pointed down to what looked from above to be no more than a great wrinkle of bark. "Under there," she said, "is a hole large enough to conceal us till night, which they will be unlikely to find. We can get down well enough with a rope of vines."

"You are sure it is large enough?"

"I lived in it for months. The question is, is it occupied now? When I found it first, there was a jaguar who thought he had better right."

"And you stayed?"

"I had no choice. He came when I was in, though I do not say I was greatly surprised, for there had been signs and scent which I could not miss. I had a gun then, and I shot before he knew I was there. But it was a narrow place, which neither could leave, and he clawed me before he died."

She looked down on her left side, where there were three long scars, giving evidence of wounds that must have uncovered the ribs, and a single deeper fissure in the soft flesh of the hip. They showed livid in the green light, and were a poor encouragement to anyone to approach that cavity in a blind way. But there is no room in the human mind for two equal fears. Far below, there came the discordant cries they had heard before. They came three times, making it certain that they were born in a man's throat. Devereux said: "I don't suppose there'll be anything there."

"Well," she answered, "you go first, if you feel like that. But you'd better have your gun ready, in case you're wrong."

He neither liked the risk nor the levity with which she passed it to him, but he saw it had to be done, and he could not ask her to lead the way. He had the vines in his hands now, their luxuriant tendrils pulled down, and tested by a sharp wrench for their strength to endure his weight. She said: "I'll be with you as quickly as I can."

Without answering, he swung out, and slid down, and entered the cleft in the tree's side, which was larger than he had expected to find. The next moment she was at his side, having been as good as her word, which was more than he had expected to see. Indeed, she being weaponless, and nude as she was, it was an act of courage which he was obliged, though none too willing to admit to his own mind.

The cavity in which they stood may have been the result of some accidental injury to the tree in its sapling days. Trivial then, it had grown with the tree's growth, until now it was a gaping wound in the huge trunk, where three or four might have sat with ease, though they could not have stood upright, except at the very edge, if they had been much more than four feet high.

"You are sure," Devereux asked, "that they won't be able to track us here?"

"Not exactly that. In the end, I've no doubt they would. But we can't be seen; nor heard if we keep quiet. When they get on our track, they'll trace our way through the trees as easily as you read a book. But there are a great many trees, and they can't get everywhere in an afternoon. Besides, they will look most on the ground. They won't think we should travel far in the trees."

"If they do that, they'll be most likely to find the boat." The thought reminded him that it was long since he had eaten last, and that he had no food with him.

"I don't know," he said, "how long it is since your last meal, but I hope we haven't got to wait till night, and then till we can find the boat in the dark, before we can get the next."

"No, you needn't do that, if they're still here."

She looked in the back of the cavity, and found some pods of Brazil nuts, which were soon broken and shared.

"There are nuts enough now in the trees," she said, "and some other things. We shouldn't starve if we were here for a month. But it was different when I got caught. For one thing, it was the opposite time of the year.... The Indians say no one need ever starve, if he will go where the monkeys go. Before I heard it, I had found out the truth of that.

"I got food of kinds while they were all about, but there came a day when they had cleared every nut from the trees, and the next they were gone.

"I'd got some stored here, as you see, but I didn't want to eat nothing else, and I knew they'd be gone long before the next crop if I did. So I tried stealing from the Indians once or twice, and if you know how they live, you'll know that it wasn't easy to do. But I had patience, and I'm not afraid of the dark. So I succeeded once or twice. I tried mostly to steal weapons, so that I could get food for myself. Then I got too bold, and got caught."

"They didn't treat you badly?"

"They didn't treat me like those of us they caught before, nor like some prisoners they brought in about ten days ago, or I shouldn't be here. Beyond that, the less said the better. By the way, there's one of their javelins lying that side. I don't suppose either of us could throw it straight, but it might be good for a poke.... No! *Take care! Stop...!* Don't you know what they are? You'd have broken it, anyway and killed me, if not yourself, more likely than not."

The javelin had been prudently laid with its point inward to the shallow back of the little cave. It was nearly six feet long, made of hard-grained wood, but very slender and frail, so that it might have snapped in a child's hand. It was pointed with a palm-spike which looked frailer yet, but it was in its weakness that its venom lay, nor was it designed for a second use.

The brittle spike was smeared with the glutinous sap of the Mavacure creeper, the cataleptic curare, which would bring those it pricked by a short road to a rigid death. The shaft was almost cut through at the top, as Devereux had observed the arrow-head to have been, so that it should snap, if not before, at the first attempt to draw the point from a poisoned wound. Being so light, a man might carry a dozen or more of these throwing darts in a bamboo case, and know that each would be death to any creature to whom it should give a wound that might be no more than a punctured skin.

As he understood this, more from her words than anything he could see in that shadowed place, where the light that entered was next to none, and moved the javelin with a greater care until he had it pointing outward, to be a menace to any approaching foe, he said: "I might have guessed that, before you explained. It is all poisons and stealth in this hateful land."

She answered more reasonably, and with words that showed that she had assimilated something of the philosophy of Indian life: "What would you expect, in a land where you could find no metal, nor any stone for a thousand miles? And what but stealth can they use, where to see five yards ahead is a wide view?"

"Well, they may suit you. I call them no better than beasts, or perhaps worse. They are beasts with a man's wits."

"They are bad enough, but they are not that. It is never foolish to understand."

The talk died in mutual resentment, as they listened to the falling water-spouts that were now pouring along the boughs, and cascading from the broad leaves of the palms, as the heavy afternoon rain beat on the forest roof. She understood the implication that she had become degraded to toleration of savage ways, and he knew that he had been told that he was lacking in sympathetic imagination, if not in brains, as a sufficient reply.

He was the first to break a foolish silence to ask: "Will they keep up the search in this rain?"

It seemed a question both reasonable in itself, and one that would take their thoughts back from themselves to the peril in which they were, but she chose to read it another way.

"How should I know better than you? You should ask an Indian that." And then, as he took her petulance without retort: "I suppose it depends upon how much they are alarmed, or determined to get me back. They must be puzzled as to what happened, or how many friends I have, Teripa and the old woman both being killed."

"They will have been told what the girls saw."

"And how much was that? And what sense will they get from them?"

He avoided the obvious reply that she should judge such questions better than he, lest he be taken to repeat the offence of a few moments before, but he saw that she had, in fact, appreciated the situation better than he had done.

He had seen only their own position, as that of two fugitives fleeing overwhelming pursuit, as in fact they were, but he had failed to see how differently the event would appear to the Indians, who would know only that the secret lodge had been discovered, its guardians killed, and its captive rescued, all of which would reasonably appear as an enterprise deliberately and successfully planned. They might well be both alarmed and circumspect in their reactions, and seeing this, he saw more clearly than before that there might have been wisdom in seeking this hidden retreat at first, leaving them mystified as to the numbers of foes that they could not find.

He changed the subject, though with a natural sequence of thought, to ask: "Do you mind telling me how you got into the Indians' hands? There seems to be nothing better to do for the next hour."

"Yes, I'll do that, if you'll tell me about yourself, which seems queerer to me."

CHAPTER NINE

JUANITA EXPLAINS

"I CAME from Manaos," she began, "about two years ago—perhaps less than that, but I can't tell to a few weeks, unless I know what date it is now."

"I don't know exactly myself. I should say it's about—"

"It doesn't matter. My uncle came up from Rio—I'd been living with him—about some rare timber for a Paris firm, which he wished to inspect himself before they were loaded up. While he was there he met a man named Fonseca, whom he didn't like, and they quarrelled at first about some business matter I didn't follow—but after that they became friendly again, and Fonseca told him of a wonderful treasure beyond the forest, that's been known of for three hundred years, but no one's been able to find. He thought it was nonsense at first, but found it was something different from that, and decided to get up an expedition to discover it, though he was told that many people had come this way, but no one ever returned.

"He said that if the spirit of the first explorers hadn't died out, people wouldn't have lived here for hundreds of years leaving the most part of the country unknown, whether it had treasure or not, and it was quite time someone made another attempt.

"So he hired about forty men—the best he could get who had been in the Amazon forests before, though, of course, not as far in them as this, anything like—and he brought no end of provisions, and arms, and things for gifts to the Indians, if they would have sense enough to be friends—and there was a machine-gun, and altogether nine loaded canoes when they set out. He said he should be sorry for any bow-and-arrow Indian's who wouldn't let him alone...."

"All the same, he shouldn't have let you come."

"You mustn't blame him for that. He meant to leave me behind. In fact he'd booked my passage back to Rio on the next boat.... But I thought it would be more fun to come, and when he'd had enough start I followed, first on the next steamer that came up the river, and then in a light canoe that could move faster than his, and caught him up when it was too late to do anything worse than scold."

"It was a mad thing to do."

"Well, I've had time enough, haven't I, to think that out for myself?"

She became silent, her mind having gone back to a tragedy of which she was slow to speak, so that he wondered whether she were offended once more, and said: "Sorry. I won't interrupt again. What happened after that?"

"Everything went quietly at first. We saw no one for weeks, and the forest was strange, but kept on being the same, till I began to think that I shouldn't have been so dull on the Rio boat.... And after that I became afraid. It didn't happen at once. It was just gradual, and it wasn't that I guessed what was coming. Not in the least. I thought, as my uncle did, that we were too strong to have reason to be afraid, and when we'd been more than two months without seeing a living man, he said he'd made a fool of himself bringing all that he did. He said it was like dynamiting an open door.

"It wasn't that I was afraid of anything that the Indians were likely to do. It was just fear of the forest itself. The vast, dark, rain-beaten forest, and the monotony of the steaming heat. As the streams up which we came grew narrower, and the trees shut out the sky, it got worse, and I'd have given anything to go back, even alone. To feel that I should be getting nearer to Rio every time that the paddle struck, instead of always further, further away. But I was ashamed to say that, and it wouldn't have been any use if I had.

"Then there came a day—it can't have been many miles from here, though I can't say that I've seen it since—I suppose you know the forest well enough to understand that—when we got stuck. The canoes grounded, and we couldn't get forward or back.

"My uncle sent out two men to search for deeper water that we might be able to reach, and whether they just got lost, or fell into the Indians' hands, we never knew, but they didn't come back. After he'd waited two days, he sent out eight more—two parties of four, going opposite ways—and they didn't come back either, and that didn't do any good to the nerves of those who were left.

"You can see how we were placed. We didn't want to abandon the canoes. According to all that was known or believed about the forest levels, and according to the map we had, it was far too early to do that. My uncle had reckoned on using up much more of the stores, and getting on perhaps another five hundred miles, before he would have to abandon everything that the men couldn't load on their own backs."

"Yes," Devereux agreed, forgetting his promised silence, "I can sympathise there. I'm just in the same fix, if I can't find a way that the boat can go. That was what brought me looking round, and both of us into this mess."

"Well, that's how it was. If the forest had been dry, it would have been different. It would have seemed more likely that we'd got to leave the canoes behind, but it was under a foot of water in many places between the trees, and it didn't seem sense to leave the canoes, and begin wading through that.

"But, against that, the bush was so rank that we couldn't see any distance away. We'd made a camp that no one would leave for a dozen yards while the ten men that had gone to search didn't come back, and we couldn't stay there for ever.

"At last, my uncle said that the only way was to go ahead, yard by yard, in what seemed the clearest direction, dragging the canoes where the water was too shallow for them to float, and trying to find a place where there was space to get through without cutting down any of the larger trees.

"We went on like that for two days, and may have changed our position by eighty yards, and with no better prospect ahead. But the second afternoon we came to a channel of water where we could float the canoes, and we paddled on for about a mile before we came to an alley where it narrowed too much for us to get through, and there, at the side, there was a *playa*—a patch of red sand at the water side—and my uncle said we'd better land, and camp there for the night.

"I should say it wasn't ten minutes later that about half of us were dying or dead. There was grumbling as soon as the men landed that something was pricking their feet, and then one of them, who knew the Indian ways, called out—it was a scream of terror that I shall never forget—that they were walking on poisoned thorns. So it was, but it was a warning that came too late.

"My uncle wasn't hurt, neither was I, though I'd been out on the sand. We had shoes too good for the thorns to pierce. There was nothing that could be done for those who were pricked. They screamed and twisted about, and were soon dead. It was a horrible sight. Those of us who were unhurt got back into the canoes, and my uncle ordered the machine-gun to be fired into the bush.

"He kept that up for some time, but I don't know that it did any good. There was a queer cry once, that some said was a monkey's and some a man's, but nothing beyond that.

"The next morning we gave up the attempt to save the canoes. Those who were left—not much more than a dozen now—loaded as much as they could bear on their own backs, while keeping their hands free, and began to cut a way through the trees. My uncle wouldn't listen to any talk of turning back, and I don't think anyone much liked the idea. There might be something better ahead, or there might not, but we knew what was behind, and were in no mood to face it again. My uncle said that the fact that men didn't return that way didn't prove they hadn't found treasure, and better lands, for no one would go through that forest twice with nothing better than Manaos at the other end…. Anyway, that's what we did. We went on.

"But the blow-pipe darts began to come at us out of the trees. Not many at once. And they are so silent that they may fall unnoticed if they don't hit anyone. The Indians didn't show themselves, not more than a glimpse once or twice. I don't think they ever do. They don't want to get killed themselves. They want to kill those who come into their land.

"I don't know that it's sense to blame them for taking care of their own skins, but to go on, day by day, seeing no one, but feeling they're round you the whole time—it's enough to make you mad before the poisoned dart enters the skin.

"My uncle was one who didn't get hit, and he kept urging us on. He said that they might stop following us any time, if we got out of their own part of the forest—whatever that might be—and he had shots fired every now and then into the trees, which made us feel we were hitting back, if it did nothing more.

"After about a week of this, there were six of us left, and a whole day had passed without anyone getting hit, and we were beginning to hope again, and then we came to a little *playa* of sand, and it was the same where we had left the canoes, though they were gone, and the dead men had been taken away.

"We knew we hadn't been able to go very far, and that we hadn't always gone in a straight line, having to get through where we best could, and you know how little you can see of the sun, but we hadn't expected that, and even my uncle found it hard to keep up the show of courage which he had done until then. He began to curse the Indians as though it were they who had made us come round, as people are said always to do when they get thoroughly lost.

"I think we went quite blindly from there, only aiming to get away. We didn't run. You can't do that in the forest. But we did the nearest we could.

"That night, we didn't even venture to hang the, hammocks, though we had found that the Indians always left us alone when it was dark. We crouched in the densest bush, half dead with fear, and with the way we'd struggled on through the damp heat, loaded up as we were.

"When the morning came, we were one less. One of the men had died of exhaustion or fright, or something else that we didn't know. We had a hurried meal before it was fully light, trying to get away before the Indians would be awake—as though there were any use in that, with the trail we left, and they coming through the trees overhead at about ten times any pace that we were able to make, and while we were eating it my uncle looked at me, and said: "I don't think they've ever shot at you, have they?"

"I said I didn't know whether they had or not, but they'd missed if so, or I shouldn't be there, and he said: 'Well, we shan't let them get you alive; you needn't be afraid about that.' He made the other men promise to shoot me any time if he were killed, and seemed to think I ought to be rather pleased at the idea by the way he talked.

"I didn't say much, and I certainly didn't want to get into the Indians' hands, but I didn't look at it quite in the same way. It made me say what I'd thought more than once before, that we couldn't be worse off, and might be better, if we should break apart, and each try to escape separately. My uncle said if anyone felt like that he was free to go; but they didn't like the idea. So he divided the loads up again, which he had to do every time anyone was killed, so that we should leave behind the things we could best spare, and we set off again.

"We hadn't gone far before we could feel the Indians were round us on every side, and another man was shot almost at once. I think they may have decided to finish us off while we were close to their own lodge, but one of them got too bold, and showed himself, and was shot, and that seemed to frighten them off, for we were left alone for the rest of the day.

"I'd been thinking hard during that march, and when we camped I lay awake, tired as I was. I hadn't been able to get the idea of escaping separately out of my mind. My uncle had said that any-one could try it who wished, though I don't suppose he'd been thinking of me.

"I couldn't feel that I was deserting them, being no particular use that I could see, and I thought that if I were to slip away it must be done in the night, both to give me a chance of not being seen by the Indians and because my uncle mightn't have been willing to let me go. He'd seemed to think that shooting me was such a tempting idea that if I proposed going off alone he might have done it at once more likely than not; and I didn't feel quite the same about it, even in the mess I was in. I don't suppose most girls would."

She paused, as though to invite his confirmation on this point of female psychology. It was a proposition that raised some doubt in his mind. He could imagine women who would think solitude in the Amazon forests, with the possible company of its savage denizens, men and reptiles and beasts, to be worse than the quick death that a bullet gives, but he had learnt to be circumspect in his replies.

"I don't suppose," he said, "any girl would be keen on being shot by her own friends, especially if they thought they could choose the time without asking her to consent. But if you ventured into the forest alone, knowing what it would be like—well, I should say it was a very brave thing to do."

"Well, that's what I did. But I can't say that I felt very brave at the time. But I'd got the idea fixed in my mind that if we stayed to-gether we should all be caught or killed in the end, even apart from the special privilege which was intended for me; but that if we broke apart in the night, one or two, if not more, might have a chance of escape, and I argued this, but it wasn't an idea that anyone else seemed to like. I'd been carrying most of the things that I specially wanted, but I had to leave some that the others would need to have, and I had to crawl about in the dark without waking the others, to find some things that were vital to have—I mean my fair share, of course—and doing that (there was no moon that night) taught me that getting away in the dark wasn't such a feasible thing. I couldn't see for a foot, and I thought that I should be likely to make a noise breaking into the bush, or splashing about, and they'd wake and all shoot at the noise, and I should get just what I was trying to miss. And besides—not being able to see a step ahead—"

"Yes. I can understand that. What did you do?"

"I waited till the light was just beginning to come, and then, as the others began to stir, I just slipped away. I knew that when I was gone a few yards I should be as much lost from them as though it were miles, and I reckoned I should still have time to get clear before the Indians were about."

She stopped, as though at the end of a finished tale and then added: "And now perhaps you'll tell me what you're supposed to be doing here."

CHAPTER TEN

THE TREE-CAVE

DEVEREUX felt that the narrative had been broken off with an abruptness that left much untold, but he recognized that it might have covered most, if not all, that she was inclined to tell, and that she had as natural a curiosity about himself as he had of her. He said: "I'm afraid my tale isn't much beside yours. I came on the same search, and it's rather curious that I was put on to the idea by the same man, but I came alone, and had no adventures at all till I got here, and the boat stuck."

"Yes. This seems to be where they begin—and generally end."

"But I don't see why they should. It must be that we turn into the wrong channel, and get stranded, which is how the trouble starts. But there must be a channel through. It isn't sense in this flat, flooded forest that there's no waterway deep enough to carry us on. Peixoto must have gone a different way, and got through. But there's nothing surprising in that, and, of course, after three hundred years the channels may not be the same."

"I don't think we need trouble about that now."

"You think they'll have found the boat?"

"No, I don't. They'd find it sooner or later, of course. But if you've left it reasonably hidden about fifty to one that they won't find it this afternoon. We both know what the forest is, and how cautious the Indians are. If we get to the boat while the moon's up—and it rises early and full tonight—we've got more than a chance that we get clear."

"I don't see how I'm to find a channel in the dark that I couldn't find in the day."

"But if you can't go forward, you can go back."

"It's not quite as simple as that, and I don't see that it would be much help if it were. I don't want go back."

"You don't mean that you still want to go on?"

The question was an exclamation in which incredulity fought with fear.

"I don't know," he answered stubbornly, "why you should think I've changed my mind in the last hour."

"But after what I've told you! And now that the Indians know! If you'd seen how they treat those that they catch alive!"

"I can imagine that. But I'm not caught, and you seem to have got away."

"But how far? And are you suggesting that we go on together to—well, heaven knows where? Can't you understand that I must get home? I suppose"—her voice of derision had a hint of nervousness, faint but still definite to perceive—"I suppose you're not going to propose shooting me too?"

"No. I'm not a Portuguese uncle. The idea hadn't occurred to me till you mention it now. But I don't want to turn back, and it isn't a fair thing to ask. Your uncle wouldn't turn back for you when he was only started a few days, or whatever it was."

She was silenced for a few seconds by this unexpected retort, but her desire was too desperate to be silenced by any argument, good or bad. She said: "That wasn't the same at all. You can see that! We thought everything would go well. And besides, I wanted to come. It's quite different now. And after all you know now it's a mad folly to try."

"I've never expected that it would be an easy thing to get through."

"Even getting back won't be that. It's not only myself. I'm thinking of you too. It would be just throwing your life away."

He made no answer, feeling that, whether he were to live or die, his enterprise had already failed. *Cherchez la femme*. He cursed fate in his heart, and all the mothers of men.

She had intuition to see that he would only be stirred to further irritation, and perhaps obstinacy, by any sentimental appeal, and she tried reason again, in what she felt to be a reasonable cause.

"It's no use quarrelling, is it? We've got to help each other, if we're to have any chance at all. Why, if I didn't help you now, I don't suppose you could find the boat in a hundred years! Not from where we are now."

He had a moment's fear, not only that she might be right, but that in the night, even with her aid, it might not be simple to do. Not knowing where he now was in relation to the boat, how could he explain it to her? But he remembered the care with which he had noted the position of the tree by which he had climbed, in relation to the loftier tree-tops that surrounded the Indian lodge.

"I don't agree," he said, "about that. Even if you would be mean enough to refuse. But I don't want to quarrel. I only say that it isn't reasonable to ask me to go back, now that I've come all this way."

She answered in better temper, seeing evidence of victory in the exasperation with which he spoke: "I'm not only asking it for myself. I think it's the only thing for you to do. And I should be glad to think we can manage that."

Without waiting for his further reply, she went on: "How did you mark the place where you left the boat?"

When he had told her that, she said: "That ought to be simple enough. But I should like a look round while the light's good, and I don't think I shall go wrong after that. There won't be much risk if I just go up and return."

The rain had ceased now, and the unseen sky above was clear to the setting sun. The feeble light that penetrated the tangled mass of tree and creeper and broad-leafed palm was somewhat increased to eyes that had become trained to the dark. She had been fumbling for the last minutes in the black rear of the hollow in which they crouched, and now that she came to the front he saw that she was clothed in the breeches which she had worn when she first escaped into the forest, and an upper garment which the half-light did not clearly define.

"I shall be back," she said, "in much less than an hour. If I'm not, you can reckon anything here is yours. I shan't want it again."

"I shouldn't go, if you feel it's as risky as that."

"Risky as what? That's only a way of talking. You'll see me again quite as soon as you want to, if not before."

She climbed out on to the vines, and disappeared into the green gloom of the leaves, and he was alone again, to consider this unexpected adventure, and to decide what he would do, so far as any decision remained to him.

She had judged rightly when she had thought that victory would be hers where their wills clashed, though he might be exasperated to open rudeness as he gave way. He knew this almost as clearly as she, and more clearly so since she had emerged in the clothes that made assertion of what she was. It had been, indeed, the subtlest argument she could use: the most potent appeal. He might refuse to go back at the call of a woman who lived in a state of nudity in the trees—but for a lady of Rio who was in danger from savage hands!

And if he should abandon his hopes, and return with her to the civilisation from which she came, would it be sure to end, even then? He knew that, if he should do that, the hope that he might dip his hands in Peixoto's treasure would be gone for ever. Not again, should he once get free, would he venture into the sombre twilights of this incredible vastness of floods and trees: this silence, season-long, through which he had come, and which must be broken, if at all, in such sinister ways. All his life now, he felt, he must remain aware of the heavy scents of the forest flowers, and the damp odours of rank decay that rose from the swamps and the lichened trunks. Always he would see in dreams the half-lights of eternal green, shot with the jewelled colours of orchid and butterfly, of parroquet and macaw, of a thousand birds that were nameless to him, whose penetrating discordant cries defied the density of the leaves. Always the long, dim vistas of the water-channels, the sluggish saurian like an ugly log in the stream, the tortoise plunging in from the bank, the lithe gliding snakes below, the clamorous festoons of the mocking monkeys above. Always he would be oppressed by this memory of unchanging months—but it was a place to which he would not return.

So it would be: and as fortune's price it might not be much to pay. As that of failure, it was to be differently weighed. But would the price be no more than that?

He knew little of the etiquettes of these half-savage, half-Latin lands, but he had a sound idea that, in spite of licentiousness of many customs and ways of life (or perhaps because of such customs would be the more accurate word) the honour of their women, of the class to which—she had never mentioned a name!—she clearly belonged, was a matter of narrow and rigid rules. Might he not be expected to wed a woman who had been his companion in the forest solitudes of the weeks to come, with the possible danger of a knife under the ribs, if he should make excuse, as he would be certain to do? Was he (to say nothing of her!) to be cursed to a lifetime of uncongeniality, or the sordidness of divorce, by this monstrously improbable chance?

He reverted to more immediate and practical issues with the thought that length of life, whether cursed or blessed, was not likely enough to deserve overmuch worry now, either for himself or for her. Yet, for the hour at least, he was free from immediate dread. The fact that—why had she not given herself a name?—that her possessions had remained undisturbed during her captivity was good assurance of that. Evidently they had caught her, however that had occurred, when she was away from her lair, which they had not guessed; and it was equally evident that the jaguar that she had killed had not been succeeded by other tenants from the animal world… The security of the place gave him an idea, which he resolved to put to her on her return.

CHAPTER ELEVEN

AN IDEA: AND JUANITA THEREON

AN hour passed, and the girl did not return, by which Devereux became the prey of conflicting fears. She had gone (as she had said) for no further purpose than to confirm her memory of the trees while the light, was good. That should have been a matter of minutes rather than hours to one who climbed with her ease and speed. Yet the hour passed, and the short tropic twilight fell, and she did not come.

Suppose she did not return? What would honour—or inclination—lead him to do? Would he be more troubled, or more relieved? He was conscious of conflicting emotions, hard to separate or define, but he could not deny to his own mind that he was listening in a sharp anxiety for a movement among the vines. Then he had a new doubt, at which anxiety changed its shape, but did not bulk less than before.

He had told her where he had left the boat. He had refused to direct its bow toward the civilisation to which she was urgent to be returned. *Suppose she should already have possessed herself of the boat, and have turned it the way she would?* Might she not justify it to her own mind as an act of sanity which she had vainly urged him to share? Might she not argue that it was no reason that she should perish because he was infatuated in pursuit of what had become an impossible goal? Was she not, on her own account of her previous action, of a disposition to go her own way, if she were dissatisfied with the decisions of her male companions as concerning herself? Most sinister memory of all, had she not actually hinted this development to a mind too dense to see into hers, when she had told him that the contents of the cave were his, if she did not promptly return?

Thinking how easily, how absurdly, he had been fooled, and facing the utter wreck of his plans if the boat should be gone, he rose with the impulse of pursuit, which was only stayed by realisation that he could never hope to find it now that the darkness fell. He would only lose himself in the blind midnight of boughs—lose both the cave that he now had, and the boat that he would not find. Lose contact also with one whose treachery was no more than a doubtful guess.

Seeing that to attempt pursuit would be worse than vain, he commenced, with the stubborn resilience of purpose which was the best asset he had, to persuade himself that it might not mean defeat though the boat were gone.

He was in a retreat that the Indians did not suspect. It was the boat that would draw their most likely chase. The boat for which a clear channel might not be easy to find. Might not her treachery be her own death, and salvation to him, who would have shared her fate had she been loyal to him?

Secure, unsuspected there, could he not gather his requirements at leisure for a further advance? Might it not, in any case, be impossible to find a channel by which the boat could make further progress in the direction which he was determined to take…?

His thoughts were broken by the sound of a rustle among the vines that were overhead. "Are you all right?" he asked, with a relief in his voice which she was quick to observe, so that she smiled within the veil of the friendly night. "I thought," he added fatuously, "I thought you would never come!"

She answered briefly: "I got drenched going up." And then, to save explanation of that remark: "It's all right. I could see just how it lies. I know the tree by which you climbed up. I could find the boat, if it's still there, by less moon than we are likely to have."

"I didn't think you would be so long."

"Neither did I. I decided to see what was happening. They've cleared the girls out of the place where I was. No doubt they've taken them to the big lodge. I could have stayed there for the night quite safely. It's a thing they wouldn't guess I should do, and it's certain that they won't go back there during the night. I think I should have done it, only I thought you would conclude something had happened that was too good to be true."

"I should have been worried enough if you hadn't come. But it sounds a silly idea, without thinking of that. Suppose they'd scattered a few of the poisoned thorns that you say they're apt to leave lying about?"

"Well, there is that. Though it's not a very likely idea. And anyway, here I am."

She was silent upon the real reason which had inclined her to the course—probably safe by its audacity—of sleeping in the deserted lodge. When she had gone out the rain had ceased, but the leaves and branches were still soaked, as were her own garments before she had climbed to the forest roof and the light of the setting sun. The wide sea of leaves steamed in the heat, so that, at first, it was little distance that she could see.

She had a prompt experience of the danger of clothes to those who dwell in the forests that are always warm, and so often wet. "If I go back," she thought, "soaking like this, and keep the things on as they are, I shall have a fever, if nothing worse, for which I shall have chosen a wrong time."

Yet she could not reconcile herself to the idea that she would discard them again in the night, and in the close company of this stranger of her own kind.

The herd-instinct controls men and women in nine-tenths of the things they do, and women more entirely than men. A few months among Indian ways had not changed her deeply from what she was, but had merely familiarised her with a new convention, in which nudity was the accepted condition, and to wear anything beyond a necklace of claws would have been to draw eyes that would otherwise pass you by.

But with the resumption of the garments she used to wear, the tyranny of older, deeper-rooted tradition had returned with a force against which she had no will to contend. Yet an ague would be most inopportune now, and if she should return to shiver in those soaked garments during the cooler hours of the night, it was what she would be likely to get.

Her best resort had been to take them off, and spread them out to the warmth of the setting sun, and as they could do with more than minutes to dry, and also because she did not intend to return, to be soaked again, until the forest had had time to relieve itself of the rain (which its upper branches, as it drained down, would largely do in the next hour), she decided to use the time for the cautious investigation which she had made.

It was true that she had hesitated upon the idea of sleeping in the deserted lodge, and that she had only put it aside when she considered that it would leave her rescuer (as she was determined that he should be) in doubt of what her long absence might mean, and that they must use the hours of the night in another way. So she had gone back to find that her garments were dry enough, where she had bound them with strands of vine to blow from the crest of a windy palm, and descended through boughs that might not be dry, but no longer poured down cascades of water at every movement a climber made....

"I've been thinking," he said, "while you were away. I don't want to turn back, and you don't want to come on with me. I don't blame you for that, but we've got to find some way out, and I thought if you were to stay here, and I were to join you as I come back—"

"*You call that an idea?*"

"Yes. I thought it was rather good."

"Well, I don't. I call it about the most ghastly nonsense I ever heard."

You lived here a good while before, and it's evident that the place hasn't been found."

"And you suppose you'd find it again?"

"I don't see why I shouldn't."

"Haven't you any idea yet of how enormous the forests are?"

"Yes. But your uncle and I seem to have come exactly the same way."

"So you might, coming up the way that the rivers lead, though I should guess that's a fluke that wouldn't happen again in a thousand years; and when you get clear of the forest, I know that you've got directions for finding your way. My uncle told me it wouldn't matter at what point he might come to the forest edge, not by a hundred miles, though he thought he could keep to the track a lot nearer than that. But coming back would be such a different thing!"

"I should have to try to come back to wherever I hide the boat."

"You might try. Much good that would be to me! But I'm not going to be left alone here. I think it's a beastly idea. Don't you think I've had enough of the hateful place...? Besides, you wouldn't come back. No one does. I should think you've learnt enough to believe that now. If you go off with the boat, I'm as bad as dead.

70

There's no chance without that. And I shouldn't care how soon it might be."

Devereux thought of asking her what hope of escape she would have had if he had not come, but he made no answer, beyond a half-articulate "Oh, damn!" which she was not foolish enough to hear. She said: "By the way, you haven't told me your name yet."

"I don't think I've had yours either."

"Mine? Oh, Juanita will do. I asked yours."

"Devereux Carsholt."

"Is it French, or what?"

"I'm English. Not French at all."

"*English?*"

"Yes. Any reason why not?"

"Only I hadn't thought of you being that. What made you come here?"

"Come to Brazil? It's rather a long tale."

"So was mine. There's no hurry for the next hour."

"I—I don't care for talking about myself, if you don't mind."

"You mean it was rude to ask. I suppose it was. But I thought, being alone here…."

"It wasn't rude in the least. But one's not always in the right mood. I daresay I shall tell you another time."

Apprehension lightened at that, and she smiled again in the friendly dark. If he thought that he might tell her another time, he must have put away the absurd, terrifying idea that she should be left alone once more where (he must surely know in his heart) they would meet no more in this endless world of a six-foot view, and ten thousand swamps, and a thousand million of trees. And if they remained together, she was resolved that they should turn their flight in the right way.

"I suppose," he asked, "it will get lighter than this?"

"Yes. But not very much. You'll find it will be darker when we get further down but it ought to be rather better where you've hidden the boat, unless the water's so narrow that the trees are closed overhead."

"Well, if you think we shall see! They don't quite do that. I suppose there's nothing to eat here, except some more of those nuts?"

"No. They're supposed to be good food."

"I prefer what I've got in the boat, when it comes to making a full meal."

"I don't suppose we should differ there. Isn't that a good reason for finding it as soon as we can?"

"Yes," he answered doubtfully. "Perhaps you can see here better than I am able to do."

CHAPTER TWELVE

SEARCH IN THE NIGHT

FEW of the evils of life are so bad as anticipation will fear, or its joys as glad. The moonlight had little power to force downward to where they were, but the vines were a tangled ladder easy to climb, and Juanita led the way upward to the forest roof, where the light was more, though there was less closeness of crowding boughs, and their distances were not always easy to judge.

Devereux followed well enough, and found at times that to slip need not be to fall far, for safety asked no more for itself than an outstretched hand.

There are those who live in the temperate zones who believe that the mammalia rule the earth, with *Homo sapiens* a long way first on the list, and in their world it is largely true. Even in Arctic seas, the great whales feed at will, with nothing but men to fear, and in the tundra the reindeer graze.

But the tropic forests are aware of a different fact. Here are moisture and heat, which the mammalia do not lightly endure, and the giant flora crowd and jostle, strangle and climb, in a war for sunlight and space and breath, in which respite and mercy are words unknown; and only the insects dispute their rule.

It is so in the Congo forests, in Papua's steaming heat, and most so of all for a million miles of the great Amazon basin—has been so for a million years, since the blue Atlantic waters retired from what had been till then a shallow, many-isleted inland sea.

Animals there are, and some lurking men, but they are furtive and few, and live by the sufferance of, or parasitically upon the branches of the real lords of the land. The foes of the great trees here are not the beavers' teeth, or the axes of men, but creatures more of

73

their own kind, the giant creepers that struggle upward, gasping for air and light in the steaming gloom, and strangle those by whose aid they climb, only to be caught and covered and choked by others that mount ever upon themselves. They strive with a fierce vitality: they grow with a visible leaping speed, dreadful to see—and the anaconda, the one great reptile that has no fear of the forest or aught it holds, unless for the crash of a falling tree, writhes and crushes and crawls in a kindred way to that which the creepers have, as though it were from them that his strength was learned....

Devereux made his way through the forest roof with a confidence that, though he might fall, it would not be far. Juanita might have had more practice than he in making a highway of tropic boughs, but he had to thank her for no more than guidance to a tree which he could have found when the morning came. He kept the pace that she set, and if she could have made more rapid progress alone, it was a thing which he did not guess.

Only once, when she turned abruptly aside, and he would have caught her up by a straighter course, did she call sharply to him to follow closely the way she came, doing him more good thereby than he would be likely to guess.

His hand had already reached to the branch of a tree that looked like any other in the black-and-white of the moon, except that it was barren of leaves, but the bark of which would have been a brilliant scarlet, facing the sun. "Not that tree! Ants!" she had called, and he had drawn back, his fingers already bitten more than once by the insects that made the *dangarana* their home, and that will be a quick death to whatever may rest on its lurid boughs.

The hardest test of judgment and skill was in the descending of the tree by which he had climbed, as the gloom deepened beneath the congregation of leaves that became damper with each foot of the downward way. But the ground was reached, and they squelched through a thick carpet of broad-leaved plants, and the mud and water in which they grew, hearing the noises around them of creatures that scuffled and splashed away as their voices startled the night, on the natures of which it might be best to turn imagination aside.

They found the boat where it had been left, and its contents appeared to be undisturbed when Devereux, having withdrawn its waterproof coverings, and groped for an electric torch, cast its light upon them.

74

"So far," he said, with satisfaction, "so good. Unless they've scattered their presents of poisoned thorns round about, and left it here with the assurance that we shan't get off alive."

"They haven't done that. I don't think they would in a spongy soil. The thorns are so tiny and frail that they need a firm surface to drive them in. They'd be more likely to be in the boat itself."

The idea, improbable though it might be, was one to be proved with care. Juanita had seen death from the poisoned thorns, and it was a memory that remained. But the closest scrutiny that could be made with the light they had disclosed no menace to hand or foot: no evidence that the boat had come under human eyes. In the faint diffused moonlight that came down through the thinner branches (which closed in some places over the narrow channel, and left at others a strip of visible sky) they entered the boat, and started on a slow blundering course. They bumped submerged roots. They grounded in half-liquid mud. They made better progress when, while he paddled slowly forward, she sat beside with an out-thrust oar to fend off whatever might oppose them out of the gloom.

So far, there was no question of where they went, which was where they must or could, with the sole purpose of placing some distance between themselves and most merciless foes before morning should dawn. When they turned, it was reluctantly back from a shallow they could not pass. Like a corralled beast, the boat blundered slowly, reluctantly back, feeling abortively right and left for a sideward escape that it could not find.

They were near the dawn, having come through a night that had been unusually free from any continuous rain, and may still have been not far from where they had begun, when they heard a calling of many ducks from what seemed to be no great distance away.

Devereux's paddle paused. "There should be water," he said, "where those ducks are."

He looked vainly in the direction of the sound A grey mist rose with the dawn, so that what increase of light there was gave visibility upwards rather than around. But it seemed that the ground in the direction from which the cries came rose clear of the water, making it a forbidding rather than a promising way.

"I know those ducks," Juanita said; "I've seen them rise more than once, if I'm right as to where we are. But I never went that far to see what it was like. The forest was lower that way, and the trees weren't any good. I mean not for nuts or fruit."

It was a reasonable explanation. Water is not an element in an Amazonian forest that anyone, unless situated as they now were, would go far to see. But the fact that the trees had been smaller was a good sign. Amazonian forests, for all their almost frantic fecundity, forced by moisture and heat, are dense rather than of a towering height. They seldom rise more than two hundred feet from the swamps where their roots are struck. And this height decreases where the ground is so low that it is flooded not only at the times when the rivers rise, but during the greater part of the year, probably because there is continual washing away of a shallow soil. Where the trees were lower was the likeliest place for them to find water sufficient to float their keel.

"I'm tempted to go to see," Devereux said. "I shouldn't go far enough to risk not getting back. I had a lesson on that. Should you mind being left for a little while?"

"Yes, I think I should. Especially as there's no need. Why not keep together? It's better than either of us getting into a mess separately."

"I thought that we might call to each other, and that you might help me in that way in getting back."

"I didn't think that we were sufficiently popular here to start making all the noise that we could."

"No. It was a silly idea. I must manage without that."

"If we both go, we shall make more mess breaking through, and the way back will be simpler to see."

"Very well. I don't suppose we shall meet anything that won't bolt. I haven't done yet. But we'd better go prepared, especially as your Indian friends may be about before long now."

He spoke lightly, feeling that the occasion needed all the encouragement for both of them that a bold front could supply. It was a simple guess that the Indians would be searching forest and stream in the next hour, and it might be doubted whether their main lodge were as much as three miles away. He took the rifle himself, and a machete to hack the path, and he handed her the loaded revolver, with the question: "I suppose you could use this?"

"My uncle gave me some practice. I can't shoot very well."

"Then, if you have to use it at all, wait till the range is short; but we'll hope there'll be no occasion to try."

Ten minutes later they had hacked and trampled their way over a rib of land that rose, though by not more than two or three feet, above the sodden area around. Here they came to a channel of water, five or ten yards in breadth, and widening on the further side in places where the ducks they had heard before rose clamorously from the reeded shallows.

The water appeared stagnant, but when Devereux cast a leaf upon it, they saw it drift steadily, though very slowly away, showing that it was part of the river system, rather than an isolated pool in the swamp.

"We've got to get the boat here somehow," he said, "before those devils find us again."

Chapter Thirteen

The Pit

FOLLOWING the track they had made, which became more firmly trampled at every passage, and could therefore be more quickly traversed, they toiled, as those will who know that their own lives are the hazard for which they play, to transfer the contents of the boat to the bank of the discovered stream.

When they had taken the most vital requirements, they emptied the boat of its remaining contents, resolving, now that the light had broadened above, and with every succeeding minute the danger increased, that they would have it on the side on which it would be ready for instant flight, before completing the transit of the supplies which it had held.

They did this with less difficulty than they had feared, and less effort than had been required for their burdened journeys before. With the boat launched on the deeper channel, and loaded with a part at least of its priceless stores, they hesitated between the desire to rescue their remaining possessions, and the natural impulse to cast off while their lives were whole.

"I suppose," Devereux said, "they might search for a week without finding us here.... I don't like to leave the tarpaulin, and if a few more tins of food.... It seems cowardly to leave them there, when there's no sign of anyone being about. But if you think it would be wiser to go—?"

"I don't think they'll be a week coming here. An hour'd be a more likely guess, before one of them spots us, though it might be a good deal longer before they would be prepared to make an attack. That is, if they're seriously bent on running us down, which I can't say, but it's more likely than not. One or other of them will pick up

78

our trail, and they won't miss it when once it's found. But it's silliest of all to waste time hesitating about what we shall do. Suppose we go back once, and bring all we can, and let the rest go?"

So this being agreed, they went back for the last time, and came overloaded with much that they were reluctant to leave if it could be saved by one final effort of strained arms, and muscles that tired in the steaming heat.

They were two-thirds of the way back when they were confronted by a collapse of the dense green wall of the path they had hacked and trodden down in their half-dozen journeys before. A giant liana, its main stem as thick as a man's leg, had sunk sideways, dragging down with it a mass of vegetation that cumbered the narrow path beyond possibility of clambering over or clearing quickly away.

Devereux, struggling on, rifle in hand, with a burdened back, and the tarpaulin upon his head, said: "We can't get through that. But it matters less than it might, because there's a clearer way round on the left. I noticed that as I bent, pushing the boat." He laid his burdens down and began to break a way round the further side of a huge trunk of which the liana had made support. He called back: "Yes. You can come on. It's quite clear ahead. It's a pity we didn't—"

He was interrupted by a sharp cry from Juanita, who had now followed him sufficiently to see that to which they had come.

"Stop!" she cried. "*Stop*! Come back. You don't understand. It's most likely—"

He had stayed his feet as she called, and was in the act of turning, but the ground beneath them was already slipping, breaking away. He got one back on to firm earth, but his balance was too far gone to regain, and her cry stopped as she heard the crash of his fall.

Next moment she bent over the edge of what she had guessed to be, and now recognised as the tapir-pit of which she had heard much talk during the last week.

"Don't move!" she called. "Don't move! Are you hurt? There's a poisoned stake."

She had laid down her own burdens, and began to pull away cautiously more of the stakes and boughs that had so cunningly covered the pit, sufficiently to give light to what was below.

"No, I don't think I'm hurt," he called back. "At least only one arm."

In the growing light that she gave, he saw the size and shape of the pit into which he had fallen. In its midst, a strong, upright, sharp-pointed stake, intended for a much larger animal than himself, had been planted too far forward for him to descend upon it as he had crashed through the outmost edge. It was very different from the flimsy weapons which the Indians used against monkeys or birds, or their human foes. The tapir, half-elephant, half-pig, and the largest mammal of a sub-continent that the forests own, has a skin which is not easy to pierce. When his heavy body should crash down through the boughs, there must be no doubt that, if it were not actually trans-fixed by the hardwood stake, it should at least not escape without a punctured hide, which was all the poison required to ensure that it would soon shudder with the spasms that precede rigor and are fol-lowed by speedy death. But there was no danger here that frail thorns would be scattered upon the floor, where the victors would hope to stand as they cut off such parts of the rich, pork-like flesh as their traditions considered fit for the food of men.

"I've hurt a wrist," Devereux said. "I'm all right beside that. But it doesn't look as though it will be easy to get out."

The pit was deep. Its sides were not merely level and smooth. They sloped upward in such a way that the top of the pit was nar-rower than the floor, a device which was intended not only to secure the capture, but to give the hunters space for manipulating their prey.

"It looks as though we shall have to break down one side to get you out," Juanita said. "What's the best tool in the boat?"

"We've got nothing better than the machete. But it wouldn't be any good. It would take a week. And I couldn't do much to help, the sides being shaped as they are."

"It wouldn't take anything like that. Not a day. And we've got to manage it somehow. You can't stay there. All the earth I broke down would fall into the pit, and you could make a heap of it, and that would get you nearer the top. And I might throw logs and things in."

"It would take more time than we've got. Do you think you could find a vine that would bear my weight, and tie it round one of the trees...? But you'd better keep further back from the edge, or you'll come in too.... *What was that call?*"

Three times there came through the murmur of forest cries that were still clamorous to the dawn, the penetrating bird-call that they had heard on the afternoon before, and which she had taught him to understand.

"I suppose that means they're getting busy again. I'd better have a look round for a good vine."

"You'd better get to the boat. It won't do me any good for them to find you here."

"Don't talk rot. I've got to get you out first."

"You haven't possible time. They may be here in three minutes if they've found which way we came, and I suppose that's what the call means. They're just calling the others up. You've time to run, and no more. How many of them are there in all?"

"Men in the lodge? About thirty. Including boys; who've been taught to shoot."

"Well, they'll get me out quicker than you'd be likely to do!" He tried to laugh, but the effort had no very genuine sound. "But we'll try to make their number a bit less before that."

She had already left the edge as he answered. He thought he heard her picking up her burdens from the ground, and her footsteps receded and died away. Could he blame her for that? Because one was trapped, should not the other escape? Any moment now, to re-main might be to be assailed with poisoned arrows or blowpipe darts, silent and deadly out of the trees. Or their foes might boldly appear, bearing the sheaves of javelins which were an equal menace of death. Actually, finding him in the pit might delay them for time enough to allow her escape, which might otherwise have been hope-less for both.

So he thought in a cold despair which would still be just, and a cold resolve that there should first be a deadly use for the bullets his rifle held, although, placed as he was, they could be of no final avail.... There was a sound of approaching steps, and her voice came from above.

"I've moved everything into the old path, and away from here, as far as I can. It's just a chance that they will see the way we went before the creeper came down, and follow us over that. That might give us time enough, though I suppose we shall lose the boat."

It should have sounded no more than a faint hope, but a faint hope may be dear when there has seemed to be none at all a short moment before. He became sanguine to absurdity in his reply: "They'd be more likely to leave the boat where it is when they'd cleared it out. We might get away in the night."

But she had gone again, so that he did not know whether she heard. He crouched on the floor of the pit, with the rifle pointed upward between his knees. It was a poor way to aim, but he thought, at so short a range, there would be no trouble for that. His left wrist was swollen and throbbing now, and the hand would be little use. Well, he must be thankful he was not hurt in a more crippling way!

Juanita's voice came, cautiously low, over the edge of the pit: "They're not far away now, so be quiet. I shall be hiding near."

They were near, but at fault, and scattered among the trees like a pack of hounds that have lost the scent on which they had been running a moment before.

They had come to the place where the boat had been launched, and had no clue to its return almost to the place where it had been at the first.

They came through the forest by whatever way might be easiest, threading the tangled growth near the ground, or wading in water and mud, or above through the higher boughs. That was no more than their customed way. They had no use for paths, which may be ambushed by foes, or scattered with poisoned thorns, or broken by such a pit as that within which Devereux fell. Had he known more of the forest ways, he would have saved himself from the danger in which he lay. A cleared path is ever one of peril for beast or man. It must be kept cleared with much toil, for it is a scar which the forest will not lightly endure, and is it likely it will have been done in a friendly way?

Juanita, crouched under a low-growing bush, the blue-green leaves of which were broader than her own back, had a moment of doubtful hope. She could see nothing, but what she heard she could understand, and the men's voices were high and shrill. No Indian will speak in a quiet voice, and a whisper is never known, though they can be as silent as death in their movements among the boughs. It was a way that the forest had. It was a place of stealth, or of raucous cries. The Soquito Indians called to each other, and their voices were like a macaw's screams.

They would always be cautious, furtive, very circumspect in avoiding the deaths they dealt; and by the way they were now exposing themselves, and their careless cries, she knew that they had read the signs of the chase aright, and were aware that it was with a solitary companion that she had fled. One whom it should be easy to slay. One who would provide legs and arms for a general meal. One who would provide a head that could be cleaned out, and treated with hot stones and sand, and a secret composition they knew, till the skull would shrink curiously under the shrivelled skin, and it would be no more than a few inches in size, with the features intact, and the hair abnormally thick on the shrunken bone. This was a hunt that they should not miss, and that should be little peril to those who had brought two or three dozens of these foolish, blundering whites to death two years before.... They might be formidable in their own lands. So they were if the tales which were told of them were true, though their noisy weapons were not much to be feared beside the deadly silence of blowpipe and bow. But here, in the forest depths that were strange to them, they blundered helplessly about, like an owl in the midday sun.

So they searched with boldness and zest, nor with lessened hope when they saw that it was by water their quarry fled, for they knew it was but a hindered way. They spread down the sides of the narrow channel, giving Juanita a half-hope that they would wander away, until she heard one calling aloud, having found the trampled track by which they had dragged the boat, and she heard the answering calls, and knew that they were gathering now, and coming fast toward where she crouched, with a heart that beat till she thought it must be heard, though she should otherwise be securely hid.

But there was still the chance that they would pursue the way that the boat had gone, and so at first it seemed it would be. They came to a blocked way, but one on which it would have been clear to eyes less expert than theirs that the dragging keel had gone on before the falling liana had closed the path.

Not being burdened with more than their weapons, and being as much at home in the trees as on ground that was rarely firm, they had made no trouble of the obstruction, swarming over and past, but one had called, with a voice that Juanita knew, and in words she could understand: "There's the tapir-pit close by. I'll have a look at it while I'm here."

The next moment she saw his legs pass as she lay hid, and crouched too low to see higher than that, and then heard his high excited scream that they had a catch in the pit.

Cautiously she looked out, not enough to be seen, but enough to see what might happen beside the pit. The man ran up to it, aware of no cause for caution. He bent over the edge. A shot came loud from the narrow mouth. He fell forward. A thin wisp of smoke drifted toward her, and dissolved in the green gloom of the leaves, and all was as before. Would the sound be unobserved? Would he be the only one who would come?

CHAPTER FOURTEEN

CONFLICT AT THE PIT

DEVEREUX heard the shouts, indistinct to him, but sufficient warning to be alert, and for his rifle to be pointed to where the covering of the pit had been broken away, when there came a crackle of branches above, and a face looked down, not in anger or fear, but with an expression gloating, expectant, anticipating the sight of a huge black body stiff in some grotesque paroxysm of poisoned death...

Tapir flesh is to be eaten with discretion, and not at all times of the year, but Okama knew that it was very good to the taste, and that he was one who would be permitted to share the feast—a matter concerning which there were rigid rules. Pregnant women might not eat it at all. So said tradition's voice in a country in which custom was iron law. Neither might women who had a child at the breast. That meant much, for the Soquito women would nurse their children for two years, if not three, during which time their husbands would provide their needs, but have no marital intercourse with them, showing in this a continence rare among men, though observed by many others of the animal world.

The women being so largely barred, there is more meat for the men when a tapir dies, and it is a beast broadly made where the meat should be, having abundance for even twenty or thirty to gorge while its freshness lasts, which will not be long. Okama looked down with a gloating face, which changed at what he saw to an instant fear. His eyes met eyes which looked up from the pit, and in a second he would have shrunk back, being a quick-witted man. But, for him, it was a second that never came. There came instead a deafening noise that he did not hear. The bullet went in under the eye, and the back of his head was broken apart. He fell forward upon the stake, upon which he remained transfixed, as the butcher-bird fixes his prey.

Devereux listened for others to come. He watched alert for other faces to peer over the edge. He listened also for any sound that might indicate that Juanita had been captured again. It was maddening to be thus confined, unable either to fight or fly. Yet for purposes of defence the pit had some advantageous points, as was proved by the last moment's event.

Juanita watched also, seeing little more, but hearing better, and with more understanding of what she heard. Her mind was active, as was natural at such a time, even to an abnormal degree. She thought that she would be caught in the end, and she thought also that she might save her life if she should give herself up in a quiet way, remembering that she had not been killed when she had been captured before. She had been kept, and treated, in intention, kindly enough, though for what ultimate purpose she could not tell, and it had not been pleasant to guess.... The Indians were kindly among themselves. They shared equally, either in plenty or want. She had not seen a child roughly treated, nor indeed punished at all. Conduct in many ways was far higher than might be observed in an English slum, or perhaps Mayfair might be compared to the same result. But the same occasions did not arise. Custom ruled; and elder and child seemed to accept it with an equal finality, and without complaint. Should a cause of dissension arise, it would be discussed in a general council, to which all, women and men, would be free to come, and its decision would have no court of appeal. Where tradition failed, public opinion ruled with an invincible force.

They had virtues, she had observed, though their practice was confined to those of their own lodge, but their virtues were not for her, and their vices had no allure.

She had seen a captured enemy killed for food, which had not been pleasant, though there had been reason in what was done. The butcher had attacked the man with a wooden sword, cutting at legs and thighs till he had brought him to the ground with bones too broken or bruised for further dodging around the fenced enclosure in which they were. Having him down, the butcher had hacked at the neck till the head was severed.

Slaughtered in this way, there would be an expression of horror on the dead face which was an important addition to the value of the head when it would have been reduced and preserved. If you have an enemy whom you capture and kill, it will be pleasant in future years to see his face contorted with horror or pain, for you know that it was through you that he suffered for what he did.

Userida, a light-skinned girl (as her name implied), with whom she had formed some degree of friendship across the difficult barriers of custom and race, had explained this, and boasted that her father, Kutino, had the most ghastly head that the lodge possessed among the trophies of more generations past than she could express in the limited vocabulary that Juanita had been able to learn.

That, fortunately for her, had been the most she had seen. For there was an impregnable law forbidding women to partake of a cannibal meal, with a certain exception for the wife of the chief man of the lodge, which was an honour as dear to her as an Ascot frock.

Juanita's thoughts went over these things, and others that are less fit to be told, with perhaps some of a gentler kind, and her mind became fixed that she would not be taken alive again. She would lie close, if she could, or if she were seen she would make what defence she might with the revolver upon which her fingers tightened spasmodically at the thought, but, live or die, she would not go back to the captivity from which she had thought that she was breaking away.

But as to making escape, either by stealth or by the weapon within her hand, what chance would there be, now that the boat would be surely gone? She knew too much of the forest to deceive herself with the hope that she could traverse its immense distances without the use of the water channels which alone divided the green masses of vegetation, which must otherwise be hacked through, step by step, so that a mile's advance might be the work of a tiring day: forests so dense that a man might starve, even with arms of precision, while surrounded by cries and movements of beast and bird that he could not see.

And there was this man who had come so strangely upon the scene, and through whom, whether for hope or despair, she lay under the broad leaves of the bush—lay so still that a snake, yellow and banded green, crawled under her ankle, and was not startled to strike or to shrink aside. She might have left him, and been comparatively safe in the moving boat. But, by nature rather than any reasoned resolve, it had been a thing that she could not do. Even if he could successfully resist the Indian attack—and she saw that, placed and armed as he was, he might not be easy to take—he would be bound to die should she leave him now. He was without water or food, and in a pit from which even an uninjured man might despair of escape....

There was no sign, no movement of life. There had been silence, sudden, absolute, from the moment that the shot had echoed dully among the trees. Such a sound at any time, under any circumstances, would have silenced the forest to a moment of listening fear. But it would have been quickly astir again, and the monkeys would have whistled and screamed, and the parroquets become voluble, discussing what it had meant. But that the silence continued was significant in another way, and Juanita, who had been still before, became so rigid that scarcely an eyelid winked. For she knew that, in the dark, close-covered shadow in which she lay, she might be invisible, even to Indian eyes, while she lay so, but if a movement should shake a leaf—! So much she had learned from those who had a technique of living as old as, and perhaps wiser than, hers, though it had developed under different skies in another way.

She knew that the Indians were, unseen and soundless, around her now; and that so they would remain until they were assured either of solitude or of the positions of those they sought, but if she could use what she had learned of their own ways, and with Mr. Carsholt out of sight in the pit—yes, there might be a chance, though it was one the probability of which she could hardly judge.

So she lay still for an hour, which she thought more. Then she was aware that two Indians had dropped silently out of the trees at no great distance from where she lay. They came past her. She could see their legs to the knee, but no more. They passed out of her sight, and came into it again in a fuller way when, with extreme caution, she moved her head, and they had drawn near to the pit. She saw them then, almost entire, between two broad overlapping leaves that were, by three inches, of different heights.

They bent over the edge. Nothing happened. Could it be that he was dead? They looked again, pointing. They had seen the body that sprawled transfixed on the poisoned stake. Could that, they thought, could some unlucky accident that had befallen the man who had charge of the tapir-pit be the whole event? They drew back, debating how it could be.

They bent over again. Two shots came, almost as one. She saw the nearer man pitch forward, and disappear in the pit. The second was hit as he was in the act of jumping back. He ran screaming into the trees, his hands clasping a shattered jaw.

But other Indians had now appeared. They came from various angles of approach, but this time they did not withdraw at the sound of shots. This time they had seen what had occurred. They thought they saw where the danger lay, and how much it was.

There were seven of them at first, as nearly as Juanita could judge from the feet she saw, and the voices of men she knew. But the bird-call sounded and four or five others joined them. She thought it likely that this would be the total of those who were on their track, for it would have been contrary to their custom for the whole manhood of the lodge to have left their daily routines to follow them, being only the two they were. It was a chase, not a war.

But it was a chase that had now cost them three casualties—as many as they would lose in five years of a warfare ever cautious to foil their foes. The fate of those who had died was half-guessed, half-told in the cries of the injured man. They saw that they had come on the track of a most dangerous beast, but it was one that was surely trapped. It had cost already five lives, if the woman be put on the list who had fallen to her own knife in Juanita's hand, when she had endeavoured to prevent her escape, and the man with the injured jaw, who must shortly be assisted to death if he should fail to find his own road, for the forest will give no life to a damaged man.

Five is a heavy toll to take from a community of less than ninety, including children and suckling babes. They had no will to increase the loss, and they debated now what they should do, their small deep-set eyes alive with cunning and cautious hate.

Juanita heard enough to understand a plan which brought cold fear to her heart. Half of them were to surround the pit at a distance safe for themselves, but which would enable them to cast javelins into its mouth. The others were to climb the surrounding trees and, with equal caution, to attack it with simultaneous discharges of arrows and blowpipe darts.

She saw that if she were to do anything to interfere with this plan, it was a matter which could not further delay. She had six shots which she could scatter among feet and legs, with a certainty of producing panic, and more disastrous results if she could shoot straight, of which she was not sure. But after that her value for any aggressive action would be at an end, and if she were captured or killed, it would not be a matter of having given Devereux time to escape.

Without her, he was almost as certainly dead, whether the Soquitos should return to the attack, or prefer to leave him alone.

As she hesitated, she remembered his admonition as he had put the weapon into her hand. If she were not sure that she could shoot straight, she should use it only at a close range. It may not have been a sufficient reason for pausing now, and, in fact, the range was not long, but it increased the hesitation which was in itself decision, for the next moment the event had resolved itself, and those whom she might have vexed had scattered into the trees, or moved further toward the pit.

After that, she had leisure enough both to blame her own inaction, and to feel the fear that suspense brings. The silence, which seemed endless, was really long, for the Indians saw much need for caution, but none for haste, and they were always of deliberate ways, which is the law of life in the Amazon lands. The caiman does not rush about, seeking a meal: the anaconda hangs a third of his length, like a giant vine, from a branching tree, waiting for whatever may come beneath. Patience and craft are the Amazon's jungle laws.

The weapons of the Indians were as silent as their own movements. There came a time when those who climbed had gained the positions they sought. It had been planned that the attack should be simultaneous, both from above and below, so that there should be no corner of the pit that should escape: no possibility that any shifting from place to place within it would avoid death. Now the discharge of missiles began, but Juanita did not know this, hearing nothing, and being able to see little from the cover in which she lay.

The men who carried javelins each had twelve, six in hand, and six in a reed-woven sheath. Of these, they were each to throw eight, and the same number of poisoned arrows and darts were to descend at the same time from the trees. The range of modern firearms might be outside their knowledge, and was of little importance where it would be hard to find a clear view of a hundred yards, either around or above; but their experience of two years before had taught them that a bullet cannot be directed upon those who are out of sight, as a dart or an arrow can; and as these weapons needed to do no more than to graze the skin to ensure speedy and horrible death, they had a reasonable hope that their enemy would not survive the fusillade to be directed upon him.

The mouth of the pit was not a mark that men who hunted daily for food, and who must starve if their aim were bad, would be likely to miss. In much less than a minute's space, nearly a hundred missiles of death, javelin, arrow and dart, had fallen from all angles into the pit. There came no sound in response: no sign that there had been any life there to destroy; but their own ways were too silent, too furtive, for that to occasion any surprise.

They waited for a few minutes, which would have been lengthened sufficiently for the poison to finish its work, but one of the Indians, who had been bolder than most in choosing the place from which his darts should be blown, came down from his perch by branches from which he could almost see into the pit, or be seen by anyone within it who might be crouched at its further side. Almost, he would have said with confidence, is not quite. But once, as a branch swayed, he must have come between Devereux and the sky, for the rifle sounded, and he lost his hold, and came head-forward to the ground, where he lay still.

The fact was that Devereux had thought out how they would be most likely to attack him, after he had shot the two who had leaned over the edge, and he had guessed sufficiently near the truth to make such provision for his own protection as the position allowed. He was in a pit with no means of covering himself except for two dead bodies which he was reluctant to use. But he reflected reasonably that to be one of three who are dead is worse than to be one living who is covered by the other two. In the interval during which the attack prepared, he had arranged two naked olive-brown bodies above his own, with his rife at reach, but scarcely ready for action, for he rightly thought that his first care must be for complete protection, rather than to be able to shoot back at foes who were unlikely to be in sight, after the fatal lessons they had received.

But he had foreseen also that after the volleys of death should cease there might soon be faces peering over the edge, with javelins in hand that they would be very ready to throw, and when the fall of the missiles ceased he had taken to the rifle again, though still with what cover he could retain, and had been ready to pick of the human fruit that had shown for a moment upon the swinging branch of the tree. There had been no difficulty about that. In his boyhood he had been taught to bring down two pheasants with right and left. He had shot snipe.

Seeing the man fall, he concluded that personal visits would cease to be an immediate probability. On the other hand, another fusillade might be a natural consequence to expect. For the time he

91

resumed the coverings which, he was interested to notice, had already taken some of the darts which had been intended for him. But no more came. Instead of that, he heard voices which were shrill in discussion, presumably of another plan of attack, though now he could not guess what it would be.

He took courage to gather the fallen missiles together, for they lay thickly upon the floor, and he knew that while they were scattered about in the half-light, a careless movement might be his end from a palm-spike prick, and as he laid them together, short and long, with their points under the sloping wall of the pit, he heard revolver-shots in rapid succession, and very near.

"Damn the devils!" he said, "they must have got the girl now." He looked up to the edge of the pit with the impulse of a rescue he was powerless to make, and relapsed with a futile curse.

CHAPTER FIFTEEN

BUT WHICH WAY NOW?

JUANITA heard the single shot, and did not know what it might mean, but the discussion which broke out afterward among the group that gathered not more than ten yards from where she lay hidden was easier to understand.

There were some who would try another cast of missiles into the pit, and others who would go back and call a full council to decide what should be done, and one only who had a plan, which was not easily heard, but which, when understood, won a general consent.

He pointed to the trunk of a tree which had fallen so lately that it had lacked time to decay (which in that climate of moisture and heat is soon done), and asked why it should not be carried toward the side of the pit, and pushed in? Why, in short, should they not fill in the pit, which might be done without being seen from below?

It was a proposition which would have made a more instant appeal in a land of rocks, or even stones of a fair size. Here there might not be found a stone even as large as a baby's thumb, though the ground should be searched for a million acres around. Yet it might be done. The plan was approved. They found the trunk to be beyond their combined strength to lift far, but it might be rolled. It could be pushed over the edge, and the weight that made it heavy to move would make it of more avail when it should be tipped in.

Juanita heard enough to understand what they proposed, which she liked less than they. She saw that Devereux was to be buried alive, or if, with agility, and sufficient luck, he should dodge the debris which would be cast into the pit, there must come a time when he would be easy to kill. She imagined him in no more than a shallow pit where he could not hide, and the Soquitos retired to bushes and trees from which they would shoot upon him from every side. Buried or no, he would be no better than dead.

The men passed, pushing the log. They were not six feet from the trembling hand in which the revolver lay. As they bent to their task, they were more visible to her than they had been before. She saw one that she had a special reason to hate, and her hand became steady upon the butt. Tilting up the barrel to aim at the highest point she could see, she pressed the trigger. To the Soquitos, it was as though an explosion came from the ground.

By good judgement or inclination, she remained hidden. She got three more shots at the flying legs, of which two went wide in the bush. But there was a man—the one at whom she had first fired—who lay still, and another whose loin-cloth was dripping blood as he lagged in the rear of flight.

When they had gone too far for a backward glance, she came out. She ran to the edge of the pit. "Are you all right?" He heard her voice before she appeared, and laid the rifle aside.

"They haven't done me any harm. What happened? Are you safe, standing there?"

"Yes, I think so. I've been under a bush only a few yards away, and I gave them rather a shock. They were sick of it before that. You've given them too many funerals for one week. The question is how soon we can get you out."

"Well, if you feel sure—"

"I'm sure for two hours at least. If they come back at all, it will be after they've talked it over with those who were not here. They didn't mean to run any risks themselves in hunting us down, and they wouldn't feel safe now, even in the trees, without eyes in their backs."

"Well, if we've got two hours we must make them do.... I only wish we'd got something to eat here, but we mustn't think about that. If only they've left the boat—"

"I should think they have. I don't see how they'd have got it away, unless there were some here who didn't come after us, which I don't believe. I'll have another try with that vine. It ought to be quicker than filling up the pit."

"Was that what they were trying to do? I should have been a goner if you hadn't stayed."

94

"I couldn't help that. I was far too frightened to go alone."

Their voices answered each other as she toiled to twist the vine in a double strand, and to knot it round the trunk of the nearest tree. They were both exhausted by lack of food after prolonged physical toil, and Devereux was becoming conscious of a throbbing and swollen arm, but the excitement of the moment sustained them to the further effort that it required.

It was not easy to mount on the swaying rope with but one hand that was fit for use, and might have been called impossible at another time, but the pit was a place he was glad to leave, and he came again to the level ground hardly conscious of how he had made ascent.

They had a renewed confidence when they saw a little pile of blowpipes, javelins and bows, which had been laid aside that two hands might be used to propel the log, and then left behind in that panic flight. They broke all but two bows, and a store of the deadly arrows, which they took, and having the assurance of those abandoned and now broken weapons they stayed to pick up the burdens that they had laid down before, and went on to find the boat as they had left it, excepting only that some of its contents had been scattered about.

"I'm afraid I can't paddle," Devereux said, "till my wrist gets a bit better than it is now."

"I used to paddle sometimes when we were coming up the river two years ago. I don't suppose I've forgotten how. If you could steer—"

"Yes. I can manage that."

"We ought to see what we can do for that arm."

"If you don't mind, we'll leave that till we're rather further away."

"I suppose you're right," she said, not unwillingly. It was still easy to imagine that there were men, not monkeys, alert in the upper boughs. She crouched in the bow of the skiff, working the paddle to right and left, clumsily at first, but Devereux had the rudder shipped, and the boat moved fast on the narrow stream.

An hour later they came to a broader water, with a more evident current.

"Which way are you steering?" she asked sharply, as the boat turned the way that the current flowed.

"You needn't worry. You win. We're for Manaos now. Can't you see that it's almost due west by the sun, and the way that the river flows?"

He felt that after all she had done—had she not stood by him and saved his life, when she could have got singly away?—he could no longer object to take her back to the civilisation which she should not have left, but there was still a bitterness in the decision which voice and words partly betrayed.

She struck with the paddle on the right hand alone, neutralising the effect of the rudder, so that the boat lay sideways upon the stream.

"Don't be silly," she said, "you know we're going the other way."

PART TWO

THE SCREAMING LAKE, BY S. FOWLER WRIGHT

CHAPTER SIXTEEN

THE FOREST ENDS

THEY went on for some weeks. But there were days which they did not count. The river to which they had come—from which it may be that both Devereux and the earlier expedition had blundered aside at a place where it spread into wide swamps which would contract again to a clearer course—remained a channel, twisting indeed, but taking them ever further into the unknown, and being, beyond easy doubt, that of which Peixoto had told.

It broadened at times into wide shallows, at others it moved with a more rapid current between evident banks, but the aspect of the country remained unchanged. Always there were the dense, impenetrable forests on either side and ahead. Always when they would climb some tree which they would choose for its greater height, they would look over the same forest roof of unending green: would look to the same horizon which gave no sign of change in the endless plain.

"It is what has been always supposed," they said, "neither less nor more. The Amazon forest is one vast valley which never changes nor lifts."

Or they would say, in another mood: "It must change at last, if we go on. The river must have a source, and though the *montanha* may be far of, at eight hundred miles by a likely guess, and we may leave it aside, yet there must be different things in the unknown country ahead, which is Europe's size. Would you see the Alps from the south of Spain? And there would be the Pyrenees before them."

It was a proof of the level land that they came to no rapids at all. The river was of a width and smoothness that allowed them, for some weeks, to hide in the day, and paddle through the darker hours (they now being two to handle the boat), even when the moon had become narrow and late to rise.

It may have been from that cause that they saw no human life, nor sign that they had been seen, until at last they came upon men who fished, and who neither withdrew in fear (seeing but two), nor reached for any weapons they may have had.

Devereux would have passed by, at the narrow distance the river allowed, but Juanita called in the Soquito tongue, and was answered in words that were partly strange, and partly what she had heard before.

In the end, they made friends in a cautious way. Devereux gave a present of salt, which he had brought for such an event, and had lost hope that he would have occasion to use, so that he had been near to leave it behind, beyond what might be required for their own use.

It was well received, and repaid with fish, and some tortoise eggs, and fruits of various kinds, leaving both parties aware that they had bought much at a little cost, by which commerce becomes an easy and pleasant game.

The river narrowed more and more as the days passed, until they must give up the habit of travelling during the night, for which it seemed that there might be less cause than before, and then there came a noon at which they were aware of an increasing volume of sound, and came, at the river's turn, to the foot of a high fall.

They tied the boat, and climbed a way by which they debated whether they would be able to drag it up, and when they looked round at the top, they were in a desolate, treeless land; and when they looked back it was upon the roof of the forest world, which, even from that small height, appeared vaster than they had seen it before. But they knew it to be more, by ten thousand times, than they were able to see.

CHAPTER SEVENTEEN

PEIXOTO'S LAND

THEY looked round, and though they had climbed no more than a few hundred feet, they knew that they were in a different land. They saw stones. The ground beneath their feet was sandy and dry, though the scene around did not suggest that they had suddenly come to an arid place, which it would not be sense to suppose. There was verdure enough. There were bushes brilliant with strange indigo-crimson flowers. But it was an easy guess that they had come to the coastline of other days. It might be a million years since Atlantic waves had swept upward to break on that sandy shore—they knew little of such estimates of the time—history of the earth, and imagination was vague—but once, in the distant past, there was a time when they might have stood there and looked over the long slow waves that had rolled from the Atlantis shore, that had been distant four thousand miles.

"Well, I'm glad we didn't," Juanita said, "for by now we should be very dead."

She looked to be a lover of life as she stood there, her slim figure clearly shown by a movement of gusty wind through the single garment she wore, and her eyes bright with the sense of a battle done, as she looked down on the conquered forests which perhaps they only and Peixoto had ever passed.

There was exhilaration in the air of this higher land for those who had lived so long in the dim-green water-aisles that were over-arched by writhing creeper and meeting bough, to be sun-stabbed, if at all, for no more than the brief hour of the middle day.

Devereux looked at her with a half-reluctant admiration, of which he supposed her to be unaware, and sudden sense of contrition and self-reproach for the insistence by which he had brought her there, even though it might have seemed to be her own choice at the last. Very dead? They might be dead enough in the next week, if they should be foolhardy to go on now. Even to turn back would be no more than a precarious chance. He saw that they held the life she loved by no more than a slender thread.

"I don't think we could get the boat up here," she said doubtfully. "Especially if your arm—"

"My arm's right enough now, and, for that matter, I think we could. But would it be any use? We've come to the forest boundary as it's shown on the map, and it's clear that Peixoto had seen what he wrote on it: "*Here you come to the stones.*" We don't know how far we've got to go, but we know which way, and it isn't any longer that of the stream, even if we could get the boat much further up it, which doesn't look like a good guess."

"Well, if we've got to leave it!—And we might be glad not to have to lose time hauling it down, if we should happen to be in a hurry when we come, back."

They returned to the foot of the fall, and sorted out what must be regarded as indispensable things, and tried what their weight would be, and reduced them to a reluctant half, and then, with more disputation and doubt, to a half again.

They hacked a space in the deepest bush into which they dragged the boat, turning it over upon their remaining possessions, with as complete water proof covering as they had. They knew that they would not be many days' journey away before the bush would have overgrown and hidden it from any but purposed search, and that even they might have some trouble to find it again—if they should ever return.

"I wish I knew," Devereux said, "how long it will take to rot in this steaming stew."

They were more conscious of the humidity of the forest air, after tasting that which blew more dryly above.

"There's nothing like finding out, when you don't know," Juanita replied, with a resolute cheerfulness. "If you think it's begun rotting already, we'd better go at once, and start fair."

So they did, finding the ascent to be a slower and harder climb now that they were burdened with weapons and food and the single hammock which, after a quarrel generous in its intention, but sustained with a foolish obstinacy, till it had not been easy to end, had been allotted to Juanita's use, while Devereux had slept in the boat in such comfort as it allowed—and a score of miscellaneous things which they would be sure to need if they did not take.

But they came at last to the head of the fall, and turned their backs on the stream, and their faces toward the mountainous ridge that the distant horizon showed.

They were not to go directly toward this ridge, but, as they were instructed in Peixoto's crudely drawn but well annotated map, they must follow the edge of the forest until "the two peaks are one," and then turn sharply to cross a hilly and barren region ("take two days' water here") at its narrowest width, after which they would soon know whether his tale were true, or fever's dream.

They went on thus for two days, and must have risen, though not at a regular slope, for the forest was now further below; and very gradually the two peaks, which must have been of a great distance and height to be seen so long with so little change, moved more closely together.

The ground at this time was sparely covered with vegetation, and there was an almost entire absence of trees, but this must have been caused by the shallow and stony soil, rather than by the altitude, which was not great, or any failure of rain.

There was an abundance of brilliantly-flowering shrubs, and there were rocky hollows green with verdure and gay with flowers. At times they would be confronted by gorges, narrow, deep, forest-choked, which they must go far round to avoid, or descend to cross, which looked much shorter, but proved to be the more laborious method, with much hacking through tangled vines, and sinking in soggy ground.

They saw no sign of mankind, nor of mammals of any size, except that once a creature, like an Asian cheetah in its lithe grace, came at the dawn, smelling round them where they had camped, and, as Devereux reached for the rifle, snarled, and bounded lightly away.

But there were butterflies beyond count, and coloured beyond belief, emerald and crimson, orange and violet and turquoise-blue. And eagles, and great hawks, and a daylight owl, would pass overhead, particularly during the morning hours, sailing out over the forest, which was the limitless ocean on the surface of which they fed, and from which they would return as the twilight neared.

They had no use for the hammock for these nights, there being no trees sufficient to bear its weight, so that they must both sleep on the ground, which was easy to do after the burdened walk of a twelve-hour day.

Twice they descended into the forest for the gathering of fruit and nuts, and the second time a wild turkey fell to Devereux's arrow, for he had become used to the Indian bow sufficiently to appreciate its advantage over the noisy rifle for short-range shots.

So they came to the place where the two peaks were in line, appearing to be but one, and here they drank as much as they could at a clear spring, and filled the only can that they had, and turned their backs to the forest, and their faces to a very desolate land.

CHAPTER EIGHTEEN

"THE TALE IS TRUE"

"IT is a safe guess," Devereux said, "that the tale is true."

They had gained a ridge from which they looked far down on a dark-green sea, as though the Amazon forests were spread beneath them again. But this sea of dark-varnished green did not stretch far out to the limit of sight of the curving earth. It was but a narrow belt of three miles, or it might be four, and beyond was water that had the look of an inland sea.

It was a lake that had no shore, within range of sight, either to the left or ahead, and the stretch of water was broken by one island alone, that lay beneath them, and not far from the shore that curved away on the right.

The island was high as it faced them, and also as it looked out to the water; so far as it could be seen; and it was of so smooth a curve, and so level a height, that it was hard to think that it could have been built by nature rather than masons' tools. Yet its colour was one, and it showed no lift of tower, no outer harbour or quay, nor any means of entrance or of approach, such as are common to the dwellings of men. It was quiet and desolate, as though it might have stood thus from the beginning of time, and its desolation was of a very sinister sort.

Its colour was a dark, very sombre grey, against the water of the lake that was strangely black, under a black sky from which, as they looked, thunder came.

"I don't care much," Juanita replied, "whether it's true or false, if only we can get something to drink."

"By the look of the sky, we shan't have to wait long for that."

They stumbled on, being stiff with toil, and exhausted by thirst and oppressive heat, until they came to an overhanging of rock, where they put their burdens down in a place that was likely to remain dry through whatever storm, and went out to turn their mouths up to the first drops of the coming rain.

As it began to fall, the air grew blacker, as though the night had descended before its time, and as the darkness increased, there came a scream from the lake, distant and faint, but with a horror which seemed of another world, as though a tortured soul cried out from the depths of hell....

The rain came in such torrents that they were glad, parched as they had been, to draw back to the shelter that they had found. It seemed now that they were at the height of the drifting cloud. They were in the midst of a deafening thunder that did not cease. The lightnings were not above, they were round them on every side.

Juanita shivered, though it was a damp oven in which they crouched, eating fragments of hoarded food, of which little remained. "I never thought," she said, "that it would be such a ghastly place. I didn't know there was such a place in the world. It makes you think you've got lost in hell."

"There's still time to turn back."

"I've been wondering whether we could get back if we were to try. You see you brought lots of food when you started out. So did we. But your food is all gone. There's nothing worth talking about left in the boat. It would make it a very different thing getting back."

He understood her mood, which it would have been easy to share. Had he been alone, he might have felt the same way. But his was the obligation of courage now—the obligation of the one who had brought her there.

"It will be a different thing getting back," he said, "in other ways, besides that. For one thing, we should go with the current in half the time. And there are two of us to paddle or row. And we know our way about now. We should be rather harder to starve. We'll get over that well enough when the time comes.... What I asked you was whether you'd like to turn back now?"

"No. We've come too far. You know that. We should be ashamed."

She thought: "What difference does it make? No one ever got back alive. We'd been told that before."

He thought he had shown some diplomacy in putting the question to her. Of course, it was too late to turn back. It would be absurd. But she might go forward with better heart if it were by her own will, rather than that he were urging her on. And he knew just how she felt, with an intuition born of the lonely intimacies of the past weeks, which had been potent with both, even though he had resolved from the first in a stubborn mind that he would not be involved with this chance-met girl of a foreign blood, so that he should be trapped to spoil his life in an alliance which it might be easy to call romance, but which sense would condemn for the shackling folly which it would be certain to be.

But they went on no further when the storm was done, for the night was near, and the drenched forest that spread beneath them was not a place into which to hasten at such an hour. They sat instead, as the tropic sun went down over forest and lake, beneath heavy retiring clouds, terra-cotta, violet, and green, and talked of what they had heard of Peixoto's tale, and whether, after these hundreds of years, they could expect that they would be met by living men akin to those that he was said to have seen before.

Here, at least, was forest, island, and lake, proving his tale to have been substanced enough, in so far that he must have come where he had said, which was itself beyond probability or previous proof. But these were the enduring things. And so also might be the treasure which he had seen, and of which he had brought something away…. And there was something else that the centuries had not changed. "*Here*," he had scrawled on the crude map, as their copy showed, "*is the lake that screams in the night.*"

It had seemed, like other things written there, or which he was said to have told, to be the fruit of a fanciful mind, casting doubt on what might have been more believed had it been set out in a balder way. But to those who had heard the scream—not in the night, indeed, but when the kindred blackness of tempest fell—it was a plea for the truth of other things he had told of strange, or nearly incredible kinds.

"I wonder," she said, "if there's anyone alive now in that ghastly place."

"Well, we shall soon know. We'll hope, if so, that they are a better brand than those who entertained you before."

It was a subject—that of the details of her life while a captive in the Soquito lodge—which, for all those weeks, she had avoided with

107

skill. She had talked with freedom of many impersonal things. She had had seemingly confidential moods. But there were things that she never told. Subjects that she would meet with steady silence, or turn adroitly aside. And among these were included her experiences during the months that she had been in the Indians' hands. If she began explaining, she had thought, she mightn't find it easy to stop. There were degradations not to be randomly told. There might be implications latent in what might seem harmless words. It was a case in which reticence would be an instinctive wisdom, even toward one of whom she knew more, and to whom her future relations might be better defined.

But now she answered as though thinking aloud; glad, perhaps, to turn the conversation from the confronting fear. "They weren't so bad in some ways. When you live with them for some time you begin to see the reasons for what they do."

"Cannibalism, for a start? I should say the reason is that they are more beasts than men."

"That was something like what Userita said. I mean that cannibalism degrades men to the level of beasts. But she used the argument the opposite way. They think it is the men who get eaten who are degraded, not those who eat.... The Soquitos hate to think they are like animals in any respect. They're far more particular than we are about that. They pull out every hair, except those on the head, simply because animals have hairs, and they hate being the same. And if a woman has twins—they go into the forest alone when it's time for a child to be born—she will come back with only one baby, having drowned the second, because some animals have more than one at a birth, and she mustn't do the same thing.

"So they argue that, as you naturally want to degrade an enemy as much as you can, you can't do better than treat him as though he were really an animal. Animals are killed by men and by each other for food. How can you insult him more than by treating him in the same way?

"Or if you take a bone from his arm and shape it into a flute, then he must make music for you when you wish, which you know he would hate to do. It's the same idea at the root.

"But the fact is that they don't do what they like at all, whether it's bad or good. They do what their fathers did, and for that reason more than everything else. They've got a technique of living even more rigid than ours, and I suppose you can defend it about as well."

108

"Sorry," he said, between earnest and jest, "I didn't mean to be rude to your friends."

She controlled an impulse of resentment to answer quietly: "They're no friends of mine. I know what it will be if they catch us as we go back. When I think of how many of them we killed!"

"What would they do if they caught us now?"

"Suppose we talk about something else? We've got troubles enough here, without thinking of that."

CHAPTER NINETEEN

PRIMEVAL FOREST

THE forest that edged the great lake may not have been more than three miles wide at this point, which is not to say that it did not extend more widely elsewhere, for the unknown land is of vast extent, as may be seen on the world's map. As it was here, it might seem narrow enough for those who had crossed a distance which, by five hundred miles, they would have found doubtful to guess; but they had cause to wish it less before they were through.

The Amazon forests had been forbidding enough, but this rose to a greater height on a richer soil, and seemed to be of a more primitive kind. It was terrible in its rank and fantastic growths: sinister in the depths of its sombre glooms. In the oppressive air of its humid heat there was a strange silence that could be heard. There was an absence of butterflies and of birds. Its orchids, if such they were, were monstrous, fantastic beyond belief. Its giant creepers reached out with obviously moving tendrils for what they might seize in their strangling grip. There were two which touched each other and visibly fought. When Devereux's machete struck off the end of a vine that trailed over the way—it would be wrong to call it a path—that they strove to break, it drew back for a yard or more with an angry writhe, so that he remained alert, with the machete raised, lest it should advance to attack him for what he did.

But it lacked sight, whatever of other senses it may have had, and did not venture a second advance where it had been so sharply repelled.

They had not been many minutes cutting and treading down the rank ferment of stalk and leaf before they were lost to the sun, and in confusion as to the way that they ought to go. The gloom increased

110

with every yard that they went forward, leaving the sunlit outskirts of the forest behind. Seeing no light either before or ahead, they could only keep a straight course by constantly retracing their trampled steps to make sure that they had not swerved. Even as they did so it would seem that the gap they had cut had become active to close, so that they had a fear, of which they joked less by inclination than will, that they might be swallowed up and for ever enclosed in this sultry gloom. Was it here and thus that men would perish who came so far?

"We can't go on here," Juanita said, "it's not like a forest, it's like a wall."

"I don't like turning. We've done too much of that already."

Devereux thrust his machete through a mass of vegetation that seemed to be of a solid density, and the blade jarred. "It's lucky," he went on, "that it didn't break. I believe a wall's what it is. It's either that or a giant tree."

He hacked now with a more definite purpose, and Juanita aided, as had become their routine, by pulling aside that which he hewed, and all else that her hands could break, or a clasp-knife cut.

"It's a wall that it is," he said, after some minutes of this work, "and a solid one too. We may have found something here that even Peixoto didn't guess."

They worked along it, probing the green curtain now right, now left, and discovered that whatever it might be was of limited size, for it did not extend, from corner to corner, for more than three yards, or perhaps four, and an upward investigation disclosed that its height did not exceed eight feet, though a layer of decayed vegetation that had formed upon it, and afforded soil for an abundance of further growth, concealed this from all but the probing blade.

When they had worked round to a third side of equal width, they gained the first indication of the nature of their discovery. Set in a deep wall, and less choked by the forest growth than they might have expected to find, was a metal gate, locked and chained and showing dimly through heavy bars a flight of stone steps that went down, but how far could be only guessed; for a black water rose, choking the shaft that did not descend directly, but at the slope that the steps required.

"It must," Devereux made a probable guess, "be a passage under the lake, which can be flooded or drained at will."

"I wonder that we can see down it as well as we do."

"I suppose our eyes are getting used to the light."

"I don't think it's only that. Aren't there fewer trees on this side? They don't come equally close."

It was an idea that needed only to be suggested for it to be recognized as evident fact. Not only around the gate, but for a long distance on either side, there was a high dim aisle dividing the trees, though they might close densely above. Beneath their feet, the vegetation was thinner, as though it sprang from a shallow soil.

"It looks," he said, "as though there's been a road here. It can't have been long ago, or the forest would have closed up more than it has."

But further investigation modified this conclusion by the discovery that under a thin carpet of humus, and the vegetation that sprawled across it or could root in a little soil, there was a pavement of stone, solid and strong, and fitted together too firmly for any seed to take root between its unmorticed joints. It was plain that this stone-paved road had once driven a way through the forest, straight and clear, though it might now be untrodden and overgrown.

The entrance to the water-tunnel was of the same stone, and the same manner of building. The blocks were of four feet square and so closely set that no mortar had been required.

Devereux examined the gate. He said: "Gold must have been cheap when they made this."

"You don't mean it's made of gold?"

"Not pure gold. It's too hard. I've no doubt it's a gold alloy."

"That's another pointer to Peixoto's tale being true."

"More or less, yes. It doesn't go far of itself. But it's certain we've come to a very interesting place."

They were interrupted by a commotion in the water at the top of the steps, out of which pushed a blunt snout. A mouth opened, showing the menace of many teeth. Small, evil eyes surveyed them for a moment, as in a natural question of what they were, and then the beast, with a surprising swiftness, launched itself at them, its snout striking heavily on the bars of the gate, which were far too close for it to pass through. They had reason to be content that the gate was strong.

They looked down on a reptile not, perhaps, larger than had been some of the great alligators of the rivers by which they came, but somewhat different in shape, and, as it seemed, of a more active malignity.

112

"I wonder," Juanita said, "how it got in. It certainly wasn't through this gate, unless it were opened for it."

"There may be a wider entrance at the other end."

"Or it may have passed in and out through the bars when it was smaller till the day came when it got stuck inside."

"If it's stuck inside, it looks as though it doesn't go short of food."

"It looks as though the passage can't have been used for as long as it's been there."

"Well, we'll hope that we shan't have to try."

They could not foresee that a day would come when even the presence of that malevolent guardian would seem inadequate reason that the passage should not be tried.

They moved to the centre of the aisle that ran straight and far through the towering trees. There were places where it was almost choked by the vegetation that pushed outward from either side, but dimly, distantly, they saw a point of light, that led Devereux to say: "If we keep along here, we shall find a way out at last."

"We don't want any more pits."

"No. We must be cautious, of course. We must look ahead. But I don't think we need fear any dangers of that kind. This isn't a path that's just been cut for a trap, or anything else. It's evidently a road that's been made long ago at a great cost, and must have been in regular use, but it looks as though it might have been left alone for hundreds of years."

"I don't think you could be sure about that. Nor a hundred days, for that matter. When you think of how fast the forest covers everything up!"

"Well, we'll say it's not in use now as it once was.... Would you like us to leave it, and begin cutting our way through again?"

"No, I can't say I should. I'd begun almost to doubt whether we should get through at all. But I'm afraid, all the same.... The Soquitos had another kind of trap, that was worse than the pit. You caught your foot in a vine, and it brought down a weight that would break your back, or loosed an arrow that would come about three feet above where your foot caught. If you found a path anywhere near their lodge, you could be sure it was for strangers, and not for their own use. But we'll agree that this one looks different, as though it might be old enough to be safe. I wonder how old it is.

113

Somehow, all the forest seems to be older than that we were in before—as though it might be part of an earlier world."

"Yes, I've noticed that," Devereux agreed; "but don't you think that may be just what it is? I mean, the forest we left—all the great Amazon valley dates from the time when the sea retired. It may be thousands of years, or millions, but it's no longer than that. But this has been land for a much longer time. This may have been a forest millions of years before, while it was near the shore of the long-gone sea. And since all that time, it may not have been cut down, or conquered by man. It's the same primeval forest, perhaps with older species of trees, even with older animals, with older insects and birds—but we don't see many of them."

"Because there aren't any to see. Suppose they're not the kind of trees on which insects thrive? They've mostly got very thick leaves, if leaves is always the right word. Suppose they're the kinds of trees that grew before the evolution of insects came?"

Devereux offered no support to this suggestion, but it was clear that they had come to a very ancient and sombre place. Slowly and cautiously, they advanced along the abandoned road, the stones of which remained potent to sterilise the surface of the earth over which they had been laid, but slow though this progress was, it was far more rapid than that at which they could have cut their way through the density of the forest thicket, and it was not long before they came to a welcome of growing light, and a glimpse of water ahead. Water lay round them also among the trees, which changed form and manner of growth, rising from clear water or swamp with flying buttresses of supporting roots.

The stone path became evident, bare, and was now a raised causeway above the sunk level of forest floor, so that they had further reason to be glad that they had stumbled upon it, and were not floundering through an impossible approach, to what must have been at last no more than deeper water and fewer trees, till they would have been confronted by open lake.

CHAPTER TWENTY

THE GREETING UPON THE QUAY

AS it was, they came out to a stone quay, which, however old it might be, was still solid and strong. Before them the lake stretched, below a grey sky of gathering storm, to a horizon that showed no shore. A wind blew toward them of sufficient strength to cause the water to beat loudly upon the quay, and to break among the trees with a lapping murmur on either hand, making a sad monotone which emphasised the stillness of all beside.

Somewhat to the right, less than two miles distant, the island lay, looking higher, larger, more imminent than they had seen it before, and it being evident now that the level circular sweep of its cliff-like wall was the work, not of Nature, but human hands, though it was still hard to see where the wall ceased, and the smoothed surface of cliff began.

But, as they came first to the open quay, they saw little of this, their eyes being drawn to the nearer sight of a row of what seemed to be enormous fantastic toads carved from a blacker stone than that of which the quay had been built, and placed at no regular intervals along its edge.

"They look filthy beasts," Devereux said, "but it's wonderful work, all the same. You can't help thinking that the sculptor must have had living creatures from which to model."

"Then they must be of enormous age, for it's certain that there are no such creatures alive on the earth now, if there ever were, which isn't easy to think."

As they talked, they approached more closely to one of these immobile images. It had a large, squat body, by the side of which that of a bullock would have seemed both graceful and small. The

115

line of its broad back, slightly sloping down to the hindquarters, was at the level of their eyes.

Devereux put a hand on the rough black side. He said: "If it weren't cold to the touch, it would be more like leather than stone. But as to how long they've been here, have you seen the pre-Inca carvings that have been dug up in Peru?"

"I've seen some queer things of the sort, but nothing quite so ghastly, and yet so lifelike as these. I think it's the way they're scattered about instead of being in an exact row that makes them so—"

She broke off sharply. She stood for a moment too paralysed by terror to move: too frightened even to scream. "Devereux," she said, using his first name, as it had not become her custom to do, even in the enforced intimacies of the past weeks, "it moved—I'm *certain*—it moved an eye."

He said quietly: "I think you're right that it's alive. I was just getting the same idea. But moving anything doesn't seem to be their strong suit. We needn't grouse about that. We'd better draw quietly away."

They withdrew to the back of the quay, content to feel that the trees were near, through which they might hope to pass more readily than these huge and clumsy bulks could be expected to do. It appeared that they had roused the one they touched, though to what emotion was not simple to guess. Very gradually, it rose somewhat upon its legs, though its belly still trailed the ground. Then, with a forward heave, it launched its seemingly reluctant bulk over the edge of the quay, splashing the water high in the sight of those who watched, though it could no longer be seen....

A voice said in Portuguese, which was good enough, though rather formally phrased: "It is the Inca's will to receive your submission now."

They turned quickly at that, being more startled than when they had found that there was life in those ponderous toads that appeared to have been left over from some older world, as though they had been too sluggish even to die. They saw a single weaponless man, dressed in scarlet and white, and having a band of upright red cockatoo feathers upon his head. He was small, elderly, lean, and had a slight stoop, as being one who bent to the pen, rather than used the sword with a lifted chin.

Devereux saw that, whatever this greeting might ultimately portend, there was no reason for present dread.

116

"The Inca's will?" he repeated. "Do you mean he already knows we are here?" He turned to Juanita to say, in a lower voice: "It gives Peixoto's tale a truer sound than before."

"If you had not been expected," the man replied, "you had not come."

He turned, as not wishing for further words, and led along the quay without looking back, as though assured that they would not delay; which indeed, having come so far, it would have been foolish to do.

They followed him, Juanita giving no sign of her thoughts, and Devereux aware of a fear which, had he allowed it to take control, would have made him a simple coward. He had to remind himself of a thought he had had when he set out, that there would be three dangers to face—the danger of coming, of being here, and of going back. Well, the way they had been accosted now was a sign that the first was done. The three perils had become two. Was there no comfort in that?

At the far right of the quay they came to a flight of stone steps, shallow and broad. Where the water beat upon them, a boat lay, in which were three men, one of whom held it to its place by a boathook, with which he had caught a ring that was in the wall. It seemed that they had been so sure that they would have only minutes to wait that they had not thought it worth while to secure themselves in a less troublesome manner. Now the man used his hook to pull the boat close to the steps.

The Inca's messenger got into it, still without looking round. He sat down on a scarlet-upholstered seat. Those who followed saw nothing better for themselves than a bare thwart, which had an ominous look, not as implying hostility so much as contempt for them, and perhaps for the race and country from which they came. The man who had come for them could be of no more worth than to be a messenger of the Inca's will, but it was seemly that he should have a better seat than was given to them.

As though aware of Devereux's thought, the man turned to him to say: "Do not think to be of greater account here than you have been in your own land. It would be to put the key in the door of death."

Devereux had time to consider this while the paddles struck, and the boat moved swiftly toward the island. It contained an unmistakable threat, with a suggestion that death could be quickly found, or might come unsought to those who were careless of where they trod. Yet he was sanguine enough to tell himself that it could be taken another way. It could be held to imply that the door of death might remain closed, if he were circumspect not to disturb its hinge. Certainly, had he been already doomed to a sure death, it would have been a warning without meaning or force, for, as the proverb says, a man need not scruple about the sheep, if he will be hanged for the lamb.

He saw also that there was reason in the argument the warning contained. It was a fact that he might have sat on a bare thwart in his own land without supposing himself to be degraded by what he did. Coming to a strange place (which he had not been invited to do) why should he expect to be treated another way? "It's safer to be meek than fierce," came to his mind, with the sound of an apposite line...

They paddled round the island until they reached that side which looked over the lake. Its apparent size had increased at a nearer view. The dark curve of its cliff-like wall was higher, grimmer, than it had appeared from the land.

They had seen no place of entrance, nor landing-ground on the shoreward side, where the wall came down to water-level, and appeared to sink sheer to a depth that it was idle to guess. They had paddled so far round that the quay from which they had come was hidden from sight when the boat was turned into a water-passage that ran into and under the wall, so that they came to a strong gate, which opened for them, and shut again, they could not see by what means.

A picture came to Devereux's mind of the London Tower, and the Traitor's Gate, with torches flashing on the dark stream, as he had seen it portrayed, while the doomed captive was handed politely out of the boat.

There was the same darkness, there were the same torches here, and here also was display of power, though it might be no more than ceremonial gesture, as he was hopeful to think. But here they had come to a strong guard, and a show of spears.

When he would have gathered the burdens which he had been glad to lay down in the boat, the guide intervened. He said: "You will not need them again," which might be true of some, but, as he hoped, not, of all.

Yet he saw that there was an element of reason in this, for he could not suppose that any sensible monarch would receive a stranger who had a bow and a sheaf of poisoned arrows beneath his arm. He might consent to be separated even from his rifle for a time, if he must, and indeed it was clear that force had become an argument on which it would be vain to rely, but he did not like the way it was put, that he would not need them again. He must hope that the guide meant no more than that the dangers and privations of the journey were over now.

So he left the boat, with his possessions still lying therein, and Juanita would have followed him out, but a man stood in her way.

Devereux turned at that. "We are not going to be separated," he said. "You must let her come."

In the haste of the moment, he spoke in English, which they would have been unlikely to understand, but tone and movement were plain enough, and it became evident that there was here a contest of wills which could have only one end. Before him was a crossing of spears.

The guide asked: "Is it for the Inca to say whom he will receive, or is it for you to decide?" There was reason here also, but the position became more ambiguous as the man added: "Besides, what is she to you? The Inca receives women at later hours."

Juanita had resumed her seat in the boat. She said: Don't do anything silly. I daresay I shall be right enough."

It did not occur to him until later that she had replied to him in his own language, which she had not used until then and which he had not supposed that she understood. He saw, with a moment's satisfaction, as they led him away, that she had the revolver in her hand, the use of which they might not understand, but there was no more than limited comfort in that, for he saw this to be a contest that might be won either through friendship or guile, but for which violence would be a less potentially.

The boat went on through the dark archway, but he was conducted up a flight of steps which, hard as they were, had been deeply dented by many feet, and then along passages and corridors of increasing size, and so to a chamber, dimly lit by a high slit in the wall, and having a table on which were dishes of fruit, and cakes of bread, and water to drink.

There were also garments upon a bench, and a laver for washing upon the floor.

The guide said: "You will find all that you need. I will return when the sun is here." He touched a mark on the wall to which the light from the window-slit might arrive in an hour's time, and went with the warning: "You must not fail to be fitly dressed, and in all things prepared by then."

CHAPTER TWENTY-ONE

THE INCA RECEIVES

DEVEREUX had time for thought, and to prepare his mind for the interview which he was to have.

Reason told him that matters, so far, had gone in a more fortunate way than it would have been prudent to hope. He had been received peaceably, and his needs had been supplied to a degree of comfort he must approve. But though reason might be content, he had an instinct that was afraid.

In the first place, there was a mystery which he did not like. How was his coming so surely known that a boat could have been put out to meet him when he arrived, and that these clothes, which were of a good fit, could have been laid out for him on the bench? The explanation might be simple—no doubt it was—but it was one he would like to know.

Then there was the separation from Juanita, on which insistence had been so firm. It might be no more than the routine of this lonely fortress court, which had remained quiescent, waiting, he supposed, an attack which had failed to come, or planning its own, which it had been too weak to launch, for three hundred somnolent years. He might find that they would be united again after the reception by the Inca Emperor for which he should be preparing now. But the doubt was an active disquiet which neither reason nor hope would still, though he reminded himself that she had not been a companion of his own will, or his own choice. The association of the past weeks, though he had been stubborn in his determination that it should not betray him to any folly such as might leave him mismated for all his life (as what else could be reasonably expected as the result of such

121

arbitrary propinquity?), had yet been potent to forge a bond which was no less strong because he would not regard it with open eyes. And, even apart from that, was there not the fact that they were two alone in this strange and potentially hostile place?

He had to ask himself also what tale he should tell the lonely monarch, who had no cause to regard him with favour, or to love the race from which he had come. It might be supposed that he would have considered this in earlier days, as perhaps he had. But the fact was that his belief in Peixoto's tale had been born of emotion and desire rather than an intellectual judgement, such as would advance to plan on a firm base. And (there was reason here) whatever Peixoto might have found, whatever his experiences might have been, were events three centuries old. Grant that his map was correct: grant that the traditions of what he told were no more and no less than true: did it follow that there would be the same things to be found today?

Was it not more likely that there would be empty ruins, long plundered by other hands? Or perhaps (since the treasure of which Peixoto told had not been known to have reached the world) a lonely place where it still lay among the bones of those who had died in an exile they had preferred to the weight of the Spaniard's yoke?

It had been a position in which it had, perhaps, been reasonable to plan, if at all, with the vagueness of dreams, until he should see what truth might be.

Now he must plan as he could while he ate, and bathed feet that were fouled with mud, and put on the white garments and golden sandals that had been laid out for his use.

He was quite alone for this hour, hearing neither voices nor steps of men, though his door, or rather his curtained archway, was wide. It was evident that it depended on his own discretion, rather than any restriction of bolt or bar, that he should not wander about. Yet it might be an easy guess that he would not go far before he would come to a closed way.

He remembered having been told that it had been a decree of the conquering Inca, Huayna Capec in the great days before the Spaniards entered the land, that no household should live with a closed, door, as their acts should be such as it would be no shame for their neighbours to oversee. And that law had prevailed, so that doors would have been hard to find throughout the wide Pacific empire he ruled, except in the mountain lands, where they would be needed to face the cold. It might be an evidence, trivial in itself, but profound in its significance, that the old traditions survived in this island fortress, remote and lonely as he supposed it to be, though they might have disappeared, or changed fundamental shape, before the impact of European civilisation in other parts of the land.

It was custom that held no threat, but it was an added warning to him that Peixoto's tale was not merely true in its own time, but had an enduring verity which he was even now destined to face. It caused him to search his mind to recall what little he knew of the character of the Inca rule, which had seemed so strong, and had fallen before a few hundred of Spanish swords. He was vaguely sure that it had been free from the bloody customs of the Aztecs in the Mexican north, but still—he wished he could have been more clear than he was that it had been incapable of sacrificing strangers to its worshipped Sun, or putting men to unpleasant deaths in more civil ways, but it seemed an unlikely hope, especially when they were aliens whose motives for coming might be more easily asked than explained in an attractive manner.

His thoughts had made little more progress than this when the Inca's messenger appeared at the entrance of the room, with two armed guards at his back.

"It is the Inca's will," he said, "to see you alone, and as not being himself, apart from which he could not converse with one too low for the exchanging of words.

"You will remember that it is not HE, and you will neither prostrate yourself, nor avert your eye from too strong a Sun, as it would otherwise be your wisdom to do. But you will remember that he sees far and all, even from when you drank with the keeper of books, and you will answer with truthful words, lest it be for you that there will be screams in the night"

Devereux heard things here which were not simple to understand, and what he understood he disliked. It was sufficiently clear that the Inca—obviously, as Peixoto had said, the descendant of the Sun-Rulers of the old Peruvian Empire—would see him incognito, which might be the mere excuse of one who had no state to display, or with a different motive which it would be his business to guess.

Obviously also, there had been some knowledge of his coming, and of the events in Manaos from which it had sprung, even to his conversations with Señor Amerigo thereon. This was surprising enough, considering the distance and isolation of the place to which

123

he had come, but he told himself again that there must be an explanation which would appear simple when he had discovered what it could be. It could mean no less—and how could it mean more?—than that those who dwelt in this remote unsuspected retreat were more aware of the civilisation from which their ancestors had fled than it was of them.

But looked at naturally, was it not reasonable, if the Inca wished his retreat to remain unknown, that he should watch the one place—Manaos—where there was a tradition of its existence, and a map, of a sort, to guide adventurous feet? And if that be allowed, rather than add new mystery, did it not rather remove that he had felt before, when he had found himself received as an expected guest?

It was his guide's concluding remark which had given him the cold shudder he must not show. Screams in the night? He thought that he knew those screams, which had not been pleasant to hear. But what did it mean that they should be for him, if the Inca should catch him in any lie? The threat was vague, but likely to dispose any man to be careful in what he said.

Busy with such thoughts, yet still alert to observe where he was led, he passed through narrow, torch-lighted passages to others that were broader, loftier, and lit through high slanting slits in the upper walls, always on his right hand, and, as he judged, opening upon an interior courtyard.

He had walked far enough to realise something of the size of this island fortress before his guide stopped at a carved door of some scented wood which was strange to him, and turned to repeat his previous warning: "You will remember that it is not the Inca to whom you speak, for the feathers are laid aside."

Next moment he stood in the presence of a man who was seated on a chair which was gaily draped and grotesquely carved, and who had a stool at his right side, on which was laid a headdress of the black-and-white vulture feathers which, from before the time when the Spaniards came, had been the symbol of Inca power.

Incognito he might be, but Devereux observed that his celestial state could be very quickly resumed.

The Inca was a small, spare man, not very dark, but having a skin tinged between yellow and red, with black hair, short and straight, and a beardless face, the hard lines of which reminded Devereux of the features of Egyptian art.

He was puzzled as to his age. There were aspects of face and figure suggesting youth, but the dark eyes in their narrow slits had a dull glazed look, as though wearied by many years.

This was the observation of a moment only, for the Inca's incognito of equality did not extend to any preliminaries of courtesy, nor to offering his visitor a seat. He commenced abruptly: "You have come far. Why are you here?"

The words were in an unknown tongue, which the one who had led him in, who now took a stand at the Inca's left, interpreted into Portuguese, as he interpreted Devereux's replies in their turn.

"There are some," Devereux fenced with discretion, "who find pleasure in wandering far."

"Where there may be things of price at the road's end? For what was it that the Spaniards first came to Cuzco with peaceful words?"

"But I am not Spanish, nor Portuguese."

"So I know. But for that you had not been here."

Devereux accepted this assurance in a silence which seemed wiser than speech. He must move slowly on a dark path, pausing as often as time allowed, or pushing forward a cautious foot.

As he was silent, the Inca spoke again: "You desire jewels and gold?"

"There are few men who do not, if they can be fairly obtained."

"You would do me service for gold? For all the gold you could bear away?"

"If you will tell me what that service could be?"

The Inca did not answer at once. He gazed at Devereux so intently with his glazed eyes as to rouse a fear that he had some hypnotic intention, so that Devereux withdrew his own eyes, as though to relieve himself from a mental assault that his instinct feared. And yet the gaze had been rather through than into his eyes, as though directed to that which was far away.

When the Inca spoke he did not reply. He said only: "Tomorrow you shall see much." He rose, as though Devereux's presence had left his mind. He said to the interpreter: "Jiros, I go to the closed room. You will give orders that none pass the guard, either in or out. I must gain wisdom before the dawn."

Devereux did not understand what was said, but he saw that he was being ignored, and that the interview was treated as being done. He saw the Inca's hand stretched toward the imperial headdress, the resumption of which might, for all he knew, make mortal treason of

125

further words. He said hurriedly: "The woman who was with me. I would know where she is. There can be no cause to keep us apart."

He had a fear as he spoke that he might be foolish, perhaps seeing trouble where none was meant, or even making it where it would not have been. It was a doubt which did not lessen as he saw that the interpreter looked perturbed, and did not translate his words, until the Inca, withdrawing his hand from the feathered insignia of power, obviously required him to do so, and then only with a brevity which must have been less than literal translation, but yet contained the substance of his request, for the Inca asked "What is the woman to you?"

"She is of my own race, and the companion with whom I came."

"I asked more than that. Is she virgin, or not?"

How could he answer that? "She is virgin, as I suppose."

"Have you come so far, knowing the people to whom you came, and not informed yourself of our customs and laws?"

"There are doubtless things that I do not know. But—"

But the Inca was in no mood for further debate. He said abruptly: "Instruct him, Jiros. It is not my will that she be mentioned again." He went out through a doorway behind his chair, the head-dress in his hand

Jiros said: "You must come back with me now. You will have further audience tomorrow, but the girl is not to be mentioned again."

"I must mention her, if she be not returned to me."

"Are you so anxious to die?"

They left the room as these words were said. Jiros spoke to the two guards who were stationed outside. One of them went, doubtless with the instructions the Inca had given. The other remained there. Jiros led Devereux back to the chamber where he had been before. The man was single and unarmed, and of little physical strength. In the long solitary passages through which they passed he would have been at Devereux's mercy had he been subjected to sudden assault. Was there not menace in the very fact that he spoke such threats, and was yet careless and unafraid?

Devereux, wondering how this might be, reminded himself that a few score of Spaniards had brought the whole Inca empire, with its twenty millions of population, to ruin and servitude in a few weeks. Why should things be different today? But he was unarmed and alone, in a place of evident strength. Beside that, he did not know that he had any cause of quarrel, or to feel ill-will.

He had heard threats, it was true; but they might be intended in a friendly and warning way. His actual reception had been good enough for one who was not an invited, and might well be an un-welcome, guest. His first need was to know more. He asked: "I suppose you have grown to be a numerous people here?"

He had not expected an affirmative answer, and was surprised to hear: "Yes. There is a great people beyond the lake."

After all, it was no more than a reasonable probability. There might have been thousands who had fled to this solitude after the final defeat, bringing their families with them. And, with the centuries, populations grow.

He changed the subject to ask: "What is this custom I should have known?"

"The Inca is the Father of all. He gives the virgins away."

"Without their consent?"

"Would they desire to refuse what the Inca wills? It would be to say that his wisdom is less than theirs. Such a one would doubtless be brought to a seemly end, but I have not known it occur. Our virgins are better taught.... And to each may be the highest honour of all."

"What is that?"

"She may be the Inca's bride of the year. She may be sacrificed to the Sun."

"I did not know that they ever had human sacrifice in Peru."

"Did you not? Yet so it was.... And customs change with the years, though, in this, it is not much. There must be homage paid to the Sun till His wrath be past, and the Incas regain their power."

"These customs may be good for you, and they are matters upon which strangers should not intrude, but they are not for women of other blood, and to whom they have not been taught."

"Are they not? She is not your wife, by your own word. Why did you bring her here? Was she not a present, such as is fit to be laid at an Inca's feet?"

"She was in a place where she could not be left, and I was un-willing to return. It had no other meaning than that."

"You have answered yourself. Those who are too week to en-dure must be at the disposal of those who can.... And she had been yours if you would. Had you made that claim, I suppose the Inca

127

might have called it good. But it would be ill for him to count you as one who will give with a grudging hand."

"Will she be safe till tomorrow?"

"Safe? Why not? I tell you she is for the Inca's disposal, which, in his own time, will be wisely done."

"Then I will speak to him tomorrow."

"And if you do, I suppose you will come to a quick end. It is a matter on which he has said he will hear no more. May not Incas choose the subjects on which they speak?"

He went away with these words for they had now come to Devereux's chamber, leaving him enough matter for thought, for the length of a sleepless night, until the hour when the daylight came.

CHAPTER TWENTY-TWO

HAPPENINGS IN THE NIGHT

DEVEREUX had come through months of physical toil, and of hours during which there must be alertness of eye and hand, but thought might pause, or move in a leisured way, and though he had been surrounded by perils of many sorts, he had slept well.

Now he had ease of body, and food that he needed neither to hunt nor snare, and strong walls around and above. His muscles rested relaxed, but his mind was active and vexed by problems it could not solve, and he could not sleep if he would.

He had come to the place he sought, which had not been easy to do, and which others had failed to reach. He found that he had been lured by no lying tale, but, by the Inca's own words, there was the treasure here which had disappeared so strangely at the Spaniards' approach, and had become the elusive doubted mirage of all the centuries since.

More than that, the Inca had given him a private immediate audience, had promised to show him the treasure, and had hinted at service he might do, and for which he was to be rewarded, to what fantastic total it would be idle to guess, so that he would soon be the owner of wealth which could be removed, not in furtive dangerous flight, but in a safe and leisurely way.

Put thus, it had a good sound, and he might be expected to sleep well, as a man will whose business prospers throughout the day. There might be ambiguities, dangers, doubts. But what had he expected to meet?

Even regarding Juanita, logic asked him in vain where his fear or his grievance lay. From the first day when she invaded his life, he had made a stubborn resolve that he would avoid being so drawn that it should become a bond that he could not break. Reason had told him that such an association with a girl whose fellowship was not choice but chance would be unlikely to be congenial when civilisation should be regained, and especially so when she was of another race and another continent than his own.

Reason told him also that if she should be kept by the Inca, willingly or unwillingly, and even given in marriage to one of these people, the responsibility was not his. It was by her own adventurous folly that she had joined her uncle's party at first. Could she blame him for that? At the worst, would she not be better off here than in savage Indian hands? Granted that she might not like to become the bride of one of the Inca race, which seemed to be her probable fate if he should cease to give her further concern, it might be much better than to have become a Soquito's mate. Even if he should claim her (which he had been told it had become too late to do), how could he even say that she would thank him for that? And what complications would it involve, both now and in days to come?

So he told himself; and when he found that such reasoning was powerless to control the restless angers and fears that drove him to pace the chamber in which he might have slept in better comfort than he had known since he had left Rio behind, he mocked himself and the perversity which only values that which is slipping beyond its reach.

Yet he remained in a mood that mockery would not still. "She is nothing," he thought, "to me. But when I fell in the pit she did not take the boat, as she might have done, saying that I was beyond help, and for the close peril in which she stood. Shall I do less for her, standing like a fool, or the coward I am, at an open door?"

Yet reason answered again, and in a way to which there was no reply. He could go out through that corridor if he would, but what did he hope to gain? To find her? It was unlikely enough. To flee with her, over the high water-surrounded walls, or through the well-guarded gate? It was fantastic to suppose that they would get away unobserved or unstayed.

Tomorrow he would learn the service the Inca sought from him and he could ask for her as for a portion of his reward. That was the safe, sensible way. Why, if he should once lose himself in this labyrinth of passages, he would not be able to explain, or to ask his way, unless he should be fortunate to meet with Jiros wandering about, which it would be absurd to expect. It might be doubted whether

Portuguese would be known to another man in the whole place! So he paced the floor as the hours passed, finding reason a barren meal.

And meanwhile the Inca, Child of the Sun, had entered his secret room, and did the one service for himself which he would not trust to another, lest he also should share his power. It was a knowledge by which a certain physician, Xanos, had thought to assure his own position, by giving it alone for the Inca's use, and had learned how foolish the wise may be.

The Inca, by the standards of those who rule, might be of just and sometimes merciful moods, but he knew that it was not right that a subject should have knowledge he did not share. He had told Xanos to show him how the drug could be truly mixed, and when the man of science refused, he had tortured him until his loyalty became of the right cast. And after that Xanos had lain two days in a dungeon with leisure to muse on the methods of those who rule, and on the obedience which is their due, the while the Inca had tested the mixing, and found that he had been truly informed. He had Xanos brought before him again, and observed, with some regret, that the tortures had damaged his body beyond repair.

"Xanos," he had said, "you have done service to me, and I would not have you live in a miserable state, having but one eye, and being twisted to such a shape. That which has been in the last week is a memory which should not endure. It is for you that the lake will scream when the moon is high."

So it had been, leaving him with a secret that no man shared.

Now he took *yagé*, which is an essence squeezed from a climbing plant that grows in the Columbian wilds. The Carijonas make a blue drink from this, and they become mad in a strange way, so that the souls of other creatures are changed for theirs. They may become pumas, going four-footed among the trees, and leaping down upon the back of a wild pig, or a cowering doe, to reach round with a claw-like hand which will tear its throat, as a puma would. Or they may become fouler creatures than that, in ways that are best unsaid.

But after some days they will return to their own kind, and will have no memory of the ways of beasts, but may be able to tell of other things they have seen, which may be from far parts of the world, of which they might say more, but that they have no suitable words, so that they will be reduced to drawing upon the ground.

The Inca took also *marihuana*, which is a cactus drug of another sort, having the property that it will make a man do that which was most in his mind when it, was drunk, though it may have been a deadly or dreadful thing, or one by which his own body will be destroyed, he being still moved by desire, but having lost all reason and all restraint.

He took cocaine, by which man may forget sorrow and lose fatigue, which might be good did not those who take it become its slaves, so that they will be no better than mad if it be withheld and if it be not they will die while their years are few.

He mixed these three in the manner that Xanos taught, and added snake-venom thereto, though no more of that than would discolour a fish-bone's point, and he had a drug which was different in its effects from any of those which had been united to give it birth.

He drank a potion of this, and having looked that his doors were barred—for an Inca may require the privacy which it is less well for his people to have—he lay down, knowing that he would sleep for twelve hours, during which time he would be in such place as he had resolved, not, indeed, in a visible bodily form, but so that he could observe that which went on, and hear what was said, excepting only that, as he had little knowledge of tongues, he was not always able to understand.

Beyond that power, of which he had permitted Jiros to know, it would give him entrance to the minds of others the while they slept, so that their thoughts and plans would be bared to a rape that they did not guess, of which he would make good use in the waking day, which was a thing that Jiros would have been startled to learn.

It was a drug which had done much service to him, showing him not only his servants' hearts, but the ways of the farther world, which his plans required him to know; but it would only serve in its own way, being of a power that even Incas could not control. He must be clear in his own mind what he would learn, and where he would go, or the results might be diverse from what he would.

He was careful not to use this drug more often than was of vital need for the plans he had, for it would be ill for these that he should be wrecked in health when the time for action should come; and, even so, he knew that his eyes were glazed, and that his hand shook at some times, and that at others he would be vexed by devils that spoke at once, saying different things at each ear.

But if he should take an extra dose (as he did now) it mattered not in what language people might talk, for their thoughts would be bare to read.

132

Now he had resolved what he would journey to see, which was not far, but why did those last words about the woman return to confuse his mind? What, in any case, is one woman, when there are millions about the world who are not always easy to tell apart in a poor light? But she had been in his thoughts, more or less, since he had observed her first in the Soquito lodge, when he had taken the drug before. Not enough to disturb his sleep, but an Inca may think much of a light desire.

All the same, she should dearly pay if she should be a cause to confuse him now! It would be an intrusion marking her for the highest honour a woman can dream to reach, so that he would hear her squeal as he put the knife to her throat, as, being not only Inca, but Priest of the Sun, it would be his office to do.

With this angry thought fixing more firmly in his mind that which he should have been calm to exclude, he settled to his drugged sleep while the evening was still young; and meanwhile Juanita waited for an event the likely tragedy of which she saw might be blamed to her, but which she had no power to prevent.

She was in a larger room than that to which Devereux had been led, with several women, old and young, whom she might regard as servants or jailers, but who showed no unkindness to her so long as she obeyed the signs she received, and yielded up the few things she had, in exchange for garments which, being clean, it was more comfort to wear.

She had only resisted the taking of the revolver with which, in so strange a place, she had been unwilling to part, but even in this she had given way almost at once when there had been efforts to wrest it from her in so careless a manner as to make it an even chance whether its contents would be discharged into her own body or that of the old woman who had one hand on the barrel and the other upon the safety catch.

At first, it had been laid aside so casually that she had hoped to possess herself of it again at a likely time, but after that it had attracted the attention of two girls who began to discuss it in words that had no meaning to her, and to handle it in such ways that she felt bound to make a vain effort to interpose, influenced alike by humanity and a reasonable expectation that the blame of any resulting tragedy would be directed to her.

Chapter Twenty-Three

Jiros Intervenes

JIROS held a precarious position in the Inca's favour, by virtue of his knowledge of certain tongues, and a supple unscrupulous adroitness in doing that which he judged him to wish, rather than in obedience of a more literal kind. But it was a quality which the Inca, being very far from a foolish man, must observe, and must weaken trust, though it might be of a value not to be cast lightly away.

But some months ago there had been a suspicion of treason, or at least of disobedience, which the Inca would not forgive. It had involved two of three, of whom Jiros was one, but which two there had been no proof, and the protests of all the three had been of the emphasis which the occasion required.

The Inca, being a just and ingenious man, had resigned verdict and punishment to higher powers even than those he derived from his Lord the Sun. He had put the three suspected men and two hungry jaguars in a pen of sufficient size to give them a short run. Two and two had made four, as they always will, and Jiros, who had been the fortunate fifth had been let out while the beasts were disembowelling those whom they had pulled down.

Jiros may have escaped because he was innocent, or because he was comparatively active and lean, but the latter is the more probable guess.

It was an incident to make the Inca watchful, and Jiros careful in all he did. He had observed the Inca's reaction to Devereux's enquiry concerning Juanita, and he had been further impressed by the questions which he had been required to answer subsequently. No one was likely to see what went on in his own mind, or to guess the motives of what he did, apart from such occult means as the Inca had, but could only sparingly use. But the issue of these deliberations was that when he had left Devereux he went to see that the girl was well treated and securely kept, which he would otherwise have been unlikely to do.

As he approached the room in which she was, he heard a loud noise, which was not thunder, being too sharp and short, and too near, but he could not think what else it might be, and he entered the room in some wonder, blended with fear, for it had been followed by an agonised scream, and then a confusion of female cries, such as men will ever find it vexing to hear.

But he entered the room boldly enough, to see a girl stretched on the floor, and pressing hands on a wound that was not easy to staunch.

There were two that attempted to give her aid, and two that shrank to the wall in a frightened way, and an old woman who had a knife in her hand with which she was advancing upon Juanita, who could do no better than look round for another weapon, having no words to be understood, and the woman being between her and the door.

The woman struck, and Juanita missed the blow by sinking rapidly to the ground in a way her assailant did not expect, and which had actually been to secure the revolver where it now lay on the floor, rather than to avoid the knife.

In another second the woman would have got a thrust in, or Juanita fired, whichever might have been first, but Jiros had a good voice, which he knew how to use, and the old woman, who had not understood what her danger was, stepped back with a bloodless knife, while Juanita, who had no will to kill her, remained still, with her finger upon a trigger she did not press.

Jiros, a quick-witted man, listened to a babel of voices, from which he guessed accurately enough what had occurred. He had never before heard a firearm discharged, but he knew what they were, having spent a time in the white man's land.

He said to the young women upon the floor: "Let her be. She will die quietly enough." He asked Juanita, in Portuguese: "Why did you do this? It might be your own way to a worse death."

He heard her account of what had occurred, which he knew to be true, for it agreed with the talk he had heard in his own tongue, which could have had no meaning for her.

He said to the old woman: "You should not have taken it from her. It has a devil if it be in other hands, but it will be quieter with her.... I will clear you of this, though it may not be easy to do. But you must keep her safe from now on, for she is one who is not far from the Inca's eye."

He turned to Juanita, who had listened to words she would have been glad to know. He said: "They will not try to take it from you again. Keep it with care. But do not think to use it for your escape, for that would be no less than your death, which is not desired."

She was surprised that it should end in this way, as she had some reason to be; but she saw that now the revolver had been demonstrated for what it was, and was left with her, she would be at more peace than before.

CHAPTER TWENTY-FOUR

THE TREASURE

THE Inca waked from his drugged sleep, and he was an angry man, less with others than with himself, that he could not rule the drug to his will, as he ruled all else in this secret empire the forest hid. He had intended to search Devereux's mind in the night, that he might judge whether he would be loyal to serve his will. That might not have been easy to do, for Devereux had had no more than short and uneasy sleep, and it is when sleep is profound that another spirit may search the records that the brain stores, feeling its convolutions and what they mean, as a blind man's fingers trace the Braille type, and gain the thoughts of others from what, in themselves, are no more than unmeaning shapes.

Devereux, falling late to a restless sleep, had once started awake in a terror he could not explain, as though an unearthly presence, an incubus of perplexing assault, had entered the room; though it was plain, by the tropic moonlight which struck down through the high slit in the wall, that there was no one there to give cause for alarm. But as he waked, there had come the high and dreadful screams of which he had heard something during the storm, and he supposed that they had sounded before, which might explain why he had waked with so strange a fear.

After that, they came again and again, loud as sirens when ships feel their frightened way through a thickening fog: piercing as though a child were in mortal pain, or a more terrible fear: sinister as though they rejoiced in a hellish way in the horror they were and did.... Hellish, that was the word. They were not of this earth at all. When once the idea entered his mind it became explanation he could not doubt. They were not of this earth at all. They were the cries of

137

souls that had strayed, by whatever means, from some distant hell. *"It is for you that the lake will scream."* What could have been the meaning of that? Was it wonderful that he did not sleep till the dawn was near?

The Inca could not recollect when he waked anything about Devereux's motives or plans that it would be useful to know, but it was evident that his wandering drug-driven spirit, being too easily rebuffed, had gone on to visit Juanita, who had been very soundly asleep by that time, having had enough to tire her during the day, and more satisfaction at last than she could have expected to get; and of her he had learnt much.

He had learnt, without much regard, the contradictions of emotion and will that may lie side by side in a woman's mind. So that she could love Devereux Carsholt for what he was, and hate him because he had not attempted that which she would have resented that he should have thought that he could do. He had been cold, where it should have been her part to repel heat: kind but cold, which, to one who felt in a warmer way, it was hard to forgive. There are states in a girl's mind where love and hate are like twin flowers on a single stem, and it is hard to say which petals will be sooner to fall. The Inca had no mind to regard this, except as it showed that the man had neglected to take a woman who had been his companion for many days. It was the gift of the drug that he had learnt this, of which he could have been as sure in no other way. It was a defect of himself that caused him to make a wrong deduction therefrom, so that he concluded that she must be repugnant to Devereux beyond the average of her kind, and that he must have misread the import of the questions that he had asked.

Apart from that, his strongest feeling was exasperation that he should have wasted the ordeal of the drug on a matter of so little account. It had done no more than to let him know that he could deal with the woman as he would (about which he was not greatly concerned) and still hope to buy the man to perform his will. And for no more than this, his head ached and his hand shook, and, at whatever need, he knew he could not venture to take the drug, even in a less strength, for some days to come. It was an annoyance which he could not put to her fault, but for which he would not be unwilling to make her pay.... The sacrifice to the Sun would be at the sixth noon from today. Well, he would make her his mistress first, which the man might think a good way to get her clear of his hands, and a re-

flected honour to him, and before the sixth day he could be gone...
It would be an escape for that plump young olive-brown Soquito
slave who would shrink and tremble when he would joke with her of
how she would feel when he would push his knife into her neck. Not
that he would forego the final pleasure of that, but it could be de-
ferred to the next year.

He sipped maté for a time, having no stomach as yet for a solid
meal, and then gave an order that those in the great audience-hall
should disperse, as he would not appear for that day, and summoned
Jiros, to whom he said: "Let there be parade forthwith of the treas-
ure-guards, and let the three keepers of the keys be released, for I
will inspect the vaults, showing the stranger the gauds I have, which
will be priceless to him."

Devereux, to whom water had been brought, and a choice of
foods, but by those with whom he could change no words, had
waited in an impatience hardly controlled until Jiros appeared.

"The Inca," he said, "will talk to you again."

Devereux replied: "I will see her first. After that, I will talk to
him."

Jiros looked at him, and did not make the Inca's mistake, having gained his knowledge another way. He answered: "It is impossible that you should do that. It would come to the Inca's ears, and we
should both die, which would be bad for us, and quite useless to her.
But I will tell you that she is well, and if you will hear the voice of a
friend, you will not speak of her to the Inca again, for you may do
more in another way."

Jiros was not a man to inspire trust, but the words had a friendly
sound, and contained an assurance that it was pleasant to hear. But
Devereux had a will that it was not easy to turn. He asked: "What do
you mean by that?"

Jiros answered: "They were plain words. If they are not enough,
they were too much, and you must suppose they have not been
said."

"I beg your pardon," Devereux replied. "I meant no more than
that I will learn all that I can."

What else was there to say? He must have a doubtful friend, or
else none....

The Inca stood with the black-and-white feathers upon his head,
which are from the tail of the great vulture which lives in the Andes

heights, and are not easy to get, nor lawful to be worn by a mortal man.

Those around him lay raised on their arms, that they might be instant to learn his will, but with their bellies scraping the ground, knowing that a god walked among men. He took the feathered crown from his head, and they rose up, one at his side receiving it on a golden tray. For the time he had condescended to become man.

He asked: "Where are the keys?" The keys came at his word, at the best pace they could make, being partly metal and partly men.

The keys were each too heavy for one man to lift, and were welded to metal girdles their keepers wore. These men trundled them forward on hand-trucks adapted to give them support. They were each lodged and guarded apart, and no key would be useful if there were less than three. The human key-bearers were somewhat distorted below the waist by the metal belts, and the great weight that they must always sustain, except so far as they could rest it when lying down, or before them upon the trucks, but they looked otherwise well, and as though they need not be replaced for a number of years. There may have been advantage in this unusual manner of securing the keys, but it may be doubted whether there had ever been adequate cause, especially if the view were sound that the Inca expressed, as he led Devereux between walls of enormous strength, their single stones being solid blocks several feet square, to gaze on treasure of gold and gem such as he had not known that the world held.

"The white races think much of these things," the Inca said, being interpreted by Jiros, as on the evening before, "and they may therefore be of value to us. But, beyond that, gold is a metal of a good colour, and durable in a soft way, but there are others of greater use; and the gems you prize are pretty trinkets for women's wear, or for days of show, but of less avail, even for such display, than are the bright feathers of birds that can be renewed at little cost as they break or soil."

Devereux did not dispute this, it being a judgment with which he was disposed to agree, as would most men of his own race, but he knew it to be an opinion of no account while women think as they do. Beside that, he was not seeking gems that he might make a chain for his own neck, or to load his fingers with rings, but to sell them as best he could. His object was not themselves, but the power they

140

would put into his hands. He thought that the less the Inca esteemed their worth, the better for him it would be likely to be.

As they paused for the unlocking of triple gates, which was a slow process, owing to the way in which the keys were attached to their human guards, the Inca gave a brief order to Jiros, who said: "I am to tell you that however much you think to see, it will be more.

"For though you may know, as the world does, that the treasure of the Incas disappeared from Cuzco, so that the Spaniards were foiled of most of the ransom they thought to take, and you may rightly suppose that you have come to the place to which it was conveyed along roads which existed then, but which the forest has long since blinded and overgrown, yet you will not suppose how enormous that treasure was, nor that it was a mere trifle beside that which had been stored here from an earlier day even from when this was not the edge of the forest-land, but an ocean coast.

"For when Atlantis was near to sink, and this land to rise, the treasure of the submerging country, which was ancient and vast, was brought by sea to the port (as it then was) and lodge in a palace here which long since fell to decay. But the treasure is here to see, with that added thereto which was brought when the Spaniards threatened the land."

Devereux listened to a tale he was not bound to believe, but that prepared him for a great sight. Yet anticipation fell far short of that which he beheld as the last gate opened, and the Inca led the way through vaults into which it seemed that shining and glowing treasures had been shot, as coal is poured through a chute. They lay heaped. They were stacked in high piles at the sides of the vaults. They were stored, not shown. They sprawled over the floor. They were underfoot. It was evident that they had not been inventoried, if at all, in any manner commensurate to their worth. And their quantity was beyond easy belief, even by one who saw.

A sack of sapphires or diamonds, a cartload of artwork in jewelled gold, might have been removed without apparent difference to what was there.

"If," Devereux said to the interpreter at his side, "the Inca values this no more than you say, it is not easy to understand why he guards it with human keys, or why it was so quickly removed from Cuzco when the Spaniards approached."

"It was removed," Jiros answered, "because it was seen to be the bait that drew them like savage hawks to the land. But you must

141

consider that, in the world's markets, all things are worth what they will fetch. It is on that matter that the Inca may wish me to say something to you."

It was at this point that the Inca paused, pointing to a casket on a small shelf, which was placed apart, as though having a special care. He said: "Show him those."

Jiros reached and opened the casket, disclosing some rows of shining stones of a rich dark colour, varying from tawny to chestnut-brown, but alike in a glowing radiance which they gave out, as though being centres of light themselves, with no debt to the sun.

"They are not diamonds," he said, "though they are equally hard. Nor do they sparkle, but give out a steadier light which is equal on every side. They were mined in Atlantis, and were there esteemed as the greatest treasure the earth has yielded to men. They were the royal stones, which only women who lay with kings might be permitted to wear. We cannot learn that they have been found elsewhere, since Atlantis was overwhelmed. Could you guess what they would be worth in today's gold?"

"No. I have little knowledge of stones. I suppose it would be a great sum."

Jiros put the casket back, and the Inca turned. He said: "We have seen enough," though there was a vault ahead that glowed richly, like a furnace of golden fire. He added: "Bring him with me."

They went out, the gates being locked again with their human keys, which the Inca paused to observe, and then went to the room where he had talked to Devereux the night before.

Here he sat again with the feathered headdress on the stool beside him and Jiros stood again as interpreter at his side.

Devereux had made a guess by this time that he was to be used for the marketing of this treasure, and it was an idea that he saw no reason to disapprove. It was a business on which the commission should be as large a fortune as greed could ask. He was very ready to hear more.

"The Inca asks," Jiros began, "whether you think there is treasure there which would buy all that a great monarch could need, though his plans were the utmost that they could be."

"I suppose," Devereux replied, "that with a small sack of those gems you could buy as much of all that the world holds as one man could desire to have. But if you should offer all, would there be no fear that the market would break...? I mean that if (shall we suppose) every man in the world were to have his pockets filled with diamonds tonight, they would be little worth on the next day."

"But if you were to feed the world through a narrow spout?"

"Then I suppose there would be few things that you could not buy."

The Inca received this reply with a satisfaction that brought a faint light to his drug-glazed eyes. He spoke to Jiros for some time while Devereux must wait in impatience, but with a mind which had become confident of the position in which he stood, for the proposition which was so clearly to come. If the Inca were requiring his aid, he would be in a position not only to make his own profit upon it, but to stipulate for the safety and release of Juanita, who (he reminded himself) might be in duress less in fact than in the apprehension of his own mind.

Jiros now turned to him to say: "The Inca chose you to come here for a purpose by which you may serve him well, and by which you may become one of the first men in the world, not only in wealth, but of a great power.

"I am to put this proposition to you, but I will first give you a warning, such as you will see could only come from a friend's mouth. It is a proposal which will place a great trust in your hands, and even to explain it, as I now shall, will be to tell you so much that if there should come a doubt to the Inca's mind, however small it might be, that you would be false, then you might live for the next week, but I think less.

"I tell you this so that you may be cautious of how you look, and not merely of what you say, as I shall explain plans that may be surprising to you."

Devereux disliked the warning, not only in itself, but for its implication that he was to be asked to do something of a dubious kind. "If," he said, "the Inca does not trust me entirely, might it not be better to leave the proposition unspoken?"

"Better for whom? It is a suggestion that might be badly received. Will you remember that it is the Inca with whom you would make debate? And, indeed, I suppose you have seen too much in the last hour to go free, except as one who has been bought to the Inca's will. You must consider why you have come here at all."

Devereux saw that he did no more than plough in a barren, and perhaps dangerous field. The Inca's gaze was upon him in an intent, dull way, which gave emphasis to the warning he had received.

"Well," he said, "go on," and then, conscious that he might appear ungracious in his reception of a hint which could hardly have been other than kindly meant, he added: "I must thank you for advice which I will not forget."

As he spoke, a new doubt entered his mind. Jiros was not one whom it would have occurred to him to trust, having a better choice. Supposing that he had been instructed to say what he had, so that he himself might be betrayed to exposure of any antipathy he might have to the coming proposition, thinking that he spoke to a friend? and whatever he said—even what he had said already—might be reported to the Inca at once. How could he tell? What measure of security could there be among men who could not understand what each other said? Now the Inca and Jiros were talking again, but he could make no guess of the substance of what they said. He saw that he would be wise to confide in nothing outside the gates of his own mind. He did not guess that even that privacy might be invaded by the arts that the Inca knew.

But now Jiros had commenced the proposal itself to which he was not likely to listen with a wandering mind.

"It has been the purpose," he said, "of the Inca, and of his fathers before him, ever since the true monarch fled and the Spaniards made of his cousin a puppet king, to regain the empire from which they had been driven without even the excuse that there was any substance of quarrel to justify the attack which had been made upon them.

"For that, an army was their first need, and one that must be of a different valour from that of the nation they ruled before, which had fled from a few hundreds of Spanish swords. To form that army they founded a settlement on the further shore of this lake where men from century to century have been taught and trained to await the hour when the white man should become weak, and their own numbers should be enough.

"But the years passed, and the time did not arrive. If their own numbers grew, so, and much more, did that of the new races that had come to possess Peru. Yet their purpose held, and it was resolved that it should not be cast aside so long as they should remain undiscovered here, as they have continued to do, having the great Amazon forests on two sides, and the unknown lake, and beyond that a desert that stretches far to the montana, which is itself little more than a wilderness land, as it climbs to the Andes heights. For they

144

said that the spirit of the white men must have become weakened from what it was when they first came, or would they have left so large a part of the land unconquered and unexplored?

"Now the present Inca, who is no more than twenty-eight years of age, though you might have guessed it at more, came to his throne two years ago, when his uncle died, and he resolved that the war, for which we have waited so many years, shall not be longer delayed. But there was no rashness in what he planned.

"He is able (which you must believe, though you may not understand) to see what is going on in other lands, even to the most distant parts of the world, and he knows that there are new methods and munitions of war which he must possess, and in the use of which he must train his troops, if they are to prevail, and it is to that end he will use this treasure, or such part of it as may be required.

"He has 400,000 men, who have been trained to hardihood and the discipline that is needed for war, and who, if they shall be fed with the coca leaves (which they are not allowed to chew largely until the time shall arrive), would have an endurance such as no white men would be likely to match.

"Surveying the present state of the world, the Inca can clearly see that the time has come. For in the first place he sees that the munitions that he requires are being made in enormous quantities, and in all parts of the world, so that he will not seek to acquire that which does not largely exist.

"He sees also that, by this manufacture of that which can only be used to destroy, all nations have become poor, so that it should not be hard to find some who will be eager to take his gold without asking too closely of whence it came.

"He sees, beyond that, that the world has become full of jealous hatreds and fears so that nations have become ripe to quarrel among themselves, and he is prepared to give wealth with a most open hand to men who will promote wars, remembering that that was how the Spaniards prevailed, both among the Aztecs and with ourselves.

"For these purposes, he must have one who can talk the languages, and will know the ways, of those to whom he will go, both to promote such discords and to purchase the munitions that he must have. And, beyond that, he must be one who is wise in the merchant's wiles, so that he can arrange for the secret transport of what he buys, and he must also obtain instructors who can train our army to use them as well as those do by whom they are made."

"It is a great deal," Devereux replied cautiously aware that his life might be quickly lost by even a look that the Inca should not approve, "for one man to undertake, and might include matters in which I could not succeed."

Jiros recommenced at this point to transmit what was said on either side, becoming merely an interpreter again. The Inca answered to this: "The magnitude of the enterprise will be transcended by its reward. And, besides, you will be free to hire all the experts you will, for whatever use, so that they will be men who can be trusted not to betray."

Devereux replied, still fencing for position, and time for thought: "If I undertake anything, great or small, it will always be a point of honour that I shall not fail. This proposal is so vast, and so unusual in all that it will require, that I should like to think of it during the night, and say tomorrow whether, and if so how best it can be contrived. If I ask this, the Inca will not take it in a wrong way?"

Jiros evidently thought that this might be put to the Inca without fear of it being misunderstood, in which he proved to be a good judge, for next moment he was able to say: "It is approved that you should consider whatever plans you may have with a scrupulous care, for it is better not to set out, than to stumble upon a wrong way. But you will do well, for all that, to be prompt in what you are deciding to do.

"For the Inca has observed that the stores of gold that have meant so much to the world since the Pizarros came to Peru, are no longer valued as once they were, even if they be counted of worth at all.

"That which was once passing from hand to hand, and so highly esteemed that men would give more of clothing or food for a pebble's weight than a man could carry away, is now idle in unentered vaults, or even buried deeply beneath the ground, from which the Inca concludes that while the value of the jewels may still endure, that of gold is a dream that is nearly done

Devereux heard an opinion with which he did no agree, and he saw opportunity to give advice both valuable and sincere, which was simpler and pleasanter use of words than to fence with them to conceal thought, with his life as the counter for which he played.

"You can reply," he said, "that the value of gold has not changed, or rather that it has increased during recent years, and though it is true that it is not circulated in coins as it once was, that

146

is rather because it has become too scarce and precious to allowed to reach the hands of private citizens who would hoard it away."

But the Inca received this explanation with obvious coldness of disbelief. He looked at Devereux with suspicious eyes. "Its value," he said, "never was, except in the imaginations of men. How should we be more prosperous here if our gold should always be passing from hand to hand? Its value to us depends upon men in other parts of the earth holding to the belief that it is of value to them, and if that delusion fail we may cast it into the lake, and shall be no poorer for what we do. And when men find that their gold may be buried away with no inconvenience to them, it is plain to see that that delusion is nearly done."

Devereux saw that he had drawn more suspicion upon himself when he had said what he believed to be true than when he had spoken with no sincerity in his heart. He reminded himself opportunely of a tale he had heard of a sailor wrecked among savage men who had won their respect by bold lying as to the wonders of the country from which he came, and of his high position therein, which they had lightly believed; but when he said that the water became solid there, so that men could walk upon it and could not sink, they recognised him for the shameless liar he was, and made him their meal of the next day.

Beyond that, he saw that the Inca spoke of that to which he had given thought, and his words had a sound of weight. Was he the looker-on who saw most of the game?

"I can assure you of this," he replied cautiously, "the value of gold has not yet declined, whatever it may be near to do. Perhaps it is that men will not easily change a belief by which they have conducted their affairs for so long a time. But it is a matter of less importance, because the jewels are far more than can be needed without the gold, and are lighter to bear."

The Inca heard this with an inscrutable face. He "I will see him tomorrow at this time. Take him away."

Chapter Twenty-Five

A Price Too High?

DEVEREUX was left alone for the rest of that day, except for the attendance of those with whom he could not exchange intelligent words.

It will be seen that he had time both for thought and sleep. Yet when the night came he slept ill, even before the moon rose and the lake screamed, and it may be supposed that he slept no better for that.

He saw that he had succeeded in the purpose for which he came, beyond the limit of hope. He could have control and possession of wealth beyond the wildest dream or imagination of man. For all he could use or desire would be no loss to the monarch, who recognised that it must be fed to the world through a narrow spout, being so much more than it would be prudent ever to cast abroad.

And the proposal must relieve him also of the greatest danger that he had supposed must be still ahead. He had thought that to find the treasure might be hard, and to possess himself of it might be harder than that, but that it might be hardest of all to bear it safely away. Even had he found it unguarded, among the derelict bones of men, he would have to return in a burdened way, very difficult to sustain.

But now, if he should pledge himself to the Inca's will, he could not doubt that there would be means provided to make his return sure, either the way he came, or through Bolivia or Peru. He would not have to flee, as Peixoto did, bearing in his body the seeds of death, and in his hand a small bag.

And against this, if he should refuse, or even hesitate in reply, he had the promise of speedy death, which he was unwilling to face.

And, not least, there was Juanita—whom he had been told not to mention again. He supposed that, if he should consent, he could stipulate for her freedom, or what he would. She could hardly be of an importance to weigh heavily against his loyalty to the Inca's plans.

He saw that the stakes could not be greater than what they were—he was offered life itself, with fantastic wealth, and a woman's honour or safety, or perhaps love, if it should be that which his folly sought. And against these, what was it precisely that he would be expected to do?

As to that, he saw that there were two questions which must be faced, and that if he could give an honest negative to the first, it might be possible to avoid the second, or to answer it in an altered form. Was that which he was asked to do possible in itself? Was it of such a nature that he could not consent, even though the price of refusal were what it was?

As to the first, his mind approached it with a willing scepticism, indicating it as the wild dream of one divorced by distance from the realities of the modern world; but as he considered it, its feasibility grew.

A huge fortune in precious stones can be packed in a small space. He did not doubt that means could be found to distribute them over the markets of the world so that they could be judiciously sold.

He knew that munitions of war were being manufactured in enormous quantities in fifty countries, large and small, in anticipation of war to come. He knew that England imposed strict control, as did some other States, over the export of arms, but he supposed that others could be found who would be more complaisant when profit spoke. Even governments, which might have become embarrassed by military expenditures, might not be unwilling to receive a few million pounds for an additional output of their national factories, without too lively a curiosity as to how the purchased arms would be consigned.

Indeed, might not the truth itself be sufficient safeguard against its own discovery? Armament firms must be used to receiving orders for destinations they were not supposed (and might be unwilling) to know. He imagined himself saying, as the order for half-a-million rifles was placed: "They are required—well, I can scarcely expect that you will believe me—but they are required by an Upper Amazon tribe." And the polite reply: "Yes, certainly. For an Upper

149

Amazon tribe. And we may suppose that it is your name only that will appear? And the payments will be in London, by bankers' draft?" He would tell the truth, and everyone would be sure that it was what he had not done.

And as to stirring up nations to the commencement of war, would it be to do more than to push fresh sticks beneath a pot that already bubbled to overflow? Let its ethics be what they were, he could not delude himself that it would be an impossible, or even a difficult thing to do, with the argument of unending gold to stimulate passions and greeds that would be in active ferment before. Doubtless, an international incident could be contrived, editors could be found who would nurse the flame.... Yes, he had to admit that he had not been asked to undertake an impossible thing.

On the ethical side, he saw also that the Inca had a strong case. His ancestors had been murdered, exiled, robbed, his people reduced to racial servitude, by those who came from the Eastern World, and this had been done without any shadow of justification, on the naked pretext that they had gold and jewels that Europe lusted to seize. But the major part of this wealth had been hidden away, and was now to be bartered for the engines of war on which Europe based its power, and they were to be used to reassert the position of those who had been injured before.

That sounded well enough, but there were two objections he could not meet. The first was that the quarrel, whether good or bad, was not his. The other was that a wrong four centuries old could not be adjusted in such a way. The Pizarros were long since dead, as were all the other adventurers who had overrun Peru. They were all gone, wrongers and wronged alike, and from their children had come a mixed race, with their own measure of freedom, their own laws, their own manner of life. They would be very unlikely to welcome the Inca as a saviour of men enslaved.

When he looked at it with a straight glance he could not see it as less than a monstrous evil which he was asked to contrive—a most monstrous evil, at an equally monstrous price.

What then was he to do? To refuse would be to bring himself, and perhaps Juanita, to speedy death.

To escape? He looked at the open porch of his room, and was tempted to try: to search for Juanita during the night (of which some hours still remained) and to seek a way out, either by violence or craft. But reason ridiculed the idea, so that, while he did not put it firmly aside, he hesitated and remained.

But if he could not escape, nor reconcile himself to the thought of death, what else was there to do? He might deceive the Inca with a promise he would not keep. It was a course by which his honour would escape, if at all, with no more than a draggled tail, but it must be allowed that his choice was hard, an one which (it may be urged) the Inca had no right to require him to make.

He resolved at last that he would agree to all that the Inca asked, escape with such jewels as should be placed in his hands, and return them—well, not all. That would be too much to expect, after he had come so far and endured so much for the glittering prize—but he would return most of them, with a letter saying that though he would not do what had been required, yet he would respect the confidence which he had received. The Inca's secret would not be disclosed, and if he should keep enough of the jewels to provide for his own wealth, it might be said that it would be no more than his silence earned, and their value to the Inca, who had so much, was just nothing at all.

He would, of course, stipulate for Juanita's freedom, which (he supposed) would be easily granted when the Inca had received assurance of his own service. And he resolved that, even to the risk of life, he would stand for that in an immovable mood, but it remained a risk of which he was not greatly afraid.

So he slept at last with the measure of peace which comes to those whose plans are made, the issue of which they must wait till the next day.

Chapter Twenty-Six

Treason—To Whom?

DEVEREUX was still engaged on the morning meal of corn-cakes and fruit which had been laid silently before him, when Jiros entered, and took an opposite seat.

Devereux was surprised, for he had supposed that the Inca would summon him at the same hour as before, and that he would be left in peace until then. Well, it seemed that events were to move more quickly today, which he did not mind.

Jiros confirmed this supposition as he came to the point with a direct question at once: "Have you decided that you can do all that the Inca requires?"

"I see nothing impossible, if it be wisely contrived."

"And it is what you are willing to do?"

"Oh, yes. I suppose I shall be so well paid that few men would refuse."

He was careful to seem quick and ready in his replies, for it was clear to his mind that Jiros was not one to trust an inch more than the occasion required, though it was also important that he should not become less than a friend, as he had shown an apparent disposition to be.

Now he received this second answer without reply. He sat looking at Devereux with a silent intentness hard to endure. It was to break this silence, rather than because he was impatient to know, that Devereux asked: "Does the Inca wish to see me at once? If so, I will come. I can leave this."

"Not at all. The Inca will receive you at the same hour as before. I came because there are things that it may be useful for you to know."

152

"I shall be glad to know all I can."

"Then I will tell you this. We had a plan some weeks ago—there were three of us in this—by which we should have opened the treasure, and made escape. It went so far that two of us—it is no matter which—had secured boats for the next night, and we had a plan for cajoling the human keys, which I should have been able to do.

"By some means which I do not know (but the Inca can see things at times beyond the range of physical sight, which gives him ever a special power) he discovered enough of this plot to know that there were two in it, who must have been of us three, but which two was beyond his power to resolve.

"So he put us to the ordeal of beasts, by which I was preserved, and my innocence thereby declared, at which you may smile, but I suppose the Inca was not unwilling that it should have come to that end, for I am most useful to him, and he may have thought that he gave me warning enough as I watched the beasts crack my companions' bones for marrow, of which I was pleased to see there was little there.

"But you will observe that I must now be most careful in all I do."

"It is a natural way," Devereux replied, "for you to feel. But I cannot see why you tell me this, which is to put yourself in my hands in a way I had not desired."

"Not at all. You may think so at the first, but if you think twice you will see that you are quite wrong. I do not trust you at all. For even if you would be believed, there is no one to tell. There is none here, excepting myself, who can either write or read in the Portuguese tongue, nor can you speak in any language they know. I can say the Inca is a crazed fool (which was what I learned when he sent me to Rio to learn your tongue), or worse things (which would still be true), and I am in no danger at all.

"But you may see further, that though I may not be in your hands, you are entirely in mine, for if I should fail to translate that which you say in such words as the Inca will be contented to hear, it would be your end, and you could not even know what I had done. So you may be pleased that, though I have no liking for him, I have a will to be friend to you."

"I have not so many friends," Devereux replied, "that I cannot do with one more. But you have not said why you have told me this, or what you would like me to do."

"I have told you that you may be frank with me, without fear. For it is important to both that we should work together."

"You may be right about that. But what is it that you propose?"

"I propose that you should appear to agree to the Inca's plans, so that he will release a great part of the wealth he has into your hands, and we will then escape together, which I can contrive, with the knowledge and power I have, so that pursuit will be vain."

Devereux considered this, which had a good appearance at first, and then a look as though it might be bad at the core.

He saw, in the first place, that there was one flaw in the argument that he could give confidence without risk to himself. Suppose that Jiros were loyal to the Inca, and this tale of his own treason no more than an invention by which confidence was to be won, so that, when he had revealed the treachery of his own heart, Jiros could return to his master to warn him that trust must not be given to one who had resolved to betray?

Considering the magnitude of the trust which the Inca was proposing to give to a stranger of alien race, was it improbable that he should give orders that he should be submitted to subtle tests, such as this might be?

He saw that an incautious word to Jiros might be the short prelude to his own end, and he saw that, whether it were the Inca or himself that Jiros sought to betray, he had spoken no more than truth when he had boasted of his own immunity and his own power.

Devereux might know him to be false to one, if not both; but it was a treachery he could not expose, unless he should try the doubtful language of signs, which would be a desperate resort in such a position as his had become; while it was plain that Jiros could bring him to a quick death if he should think well, either in the Inca's interest or his own. He could accuse him to the Inca of what he would, and there would be no possibility of reply, nor even to learn the reason of why he died.

So he thought, while Jiros remained silent, as though willing to give him time to consider the plan, and other aspects of how he stood. He saw that he must say something, and asked a question from which his own intention would not be easy to judge: "Can you tell me how I should be better off, if I should join you in such a plan, than if I should accept the Inca's offer in a more genuine way?"

"Yes, I think I could," Jiros replied. "But the trouble is that you are afraid to give me your trust, which is a dividing ditch we must first fill. How can I do that?"

Devereux heard a question to which he found no instant reply, and, as he remained quiet, Jiros, after a pause of thought, described what had occurred on the first night, and how he had befriended Juanita, so that she had not only escaped blame for the girl's death (which might easily have been twisted another way), but had found the revolver restored to her hands.

"I did that," Jiros concluded, "because I am one who looks forward to future days."

Devereux saw that it was an incident (if it were truly told) that supported the professions of friendship that Jiros made. Apart from that, it was what he was glad to hear, being the first definite news of Juanita's welfare that he had had since they had been forced apart. He asked: "May I see the girl?"

Jiros hesitated. "There may be more risk in that than you will suppose. But yes, I will contrive that, if I must. For I must find some way to make you trust me more than you are inclined to do."

"Could you get me my rifle back? It is a weapon by which there might be an accident such as that by which the girl died."

"Yes. I can do that."

"I would thank you for that. And you must not think that I am unwilling to give you trust. As I have said, I lack friends. But I will ask you the same question again, so that we may understand each other without reserve. I can see that I may be useful to your own plans, if you would escape and take a great treasure away, for the Inca might not be willing to allow you to go, and would only release the treasure to me. But what I ask is what I am supposed to gain by a secret flight, when I might accept the offer the Inca makes and go safely away?"

"You think," Jiros asked, "that you might agree to that which the Inca requires, and break your word when you had gone?"

"I did not say that. Why should I not do what I am asked? But whether my word be broken or kept, I want you to see that you ask me to take a risk that I need not have."

"So you think. But do you value the girl?"

"Yes. You have seen that. But if I agree to all that the Inca asks, he will surely let me take her away. Why should he not? And I can make it a condition of what I do."

"And I can tell you, you never will. If you make it so great a point, you will destroy both yourself and her. He thinks now that she is little to you, which it is your safety not to deny.

"If he should know the truth, it is as a hostage he would regard her, if he should trust you further at all. He might let you keep her here in a safety that would continue while you should please him in what you do. I cannot say about that. He has cruel, difficult moods in which he will do things that he will regret in a wiser hour. She might be safe. It would be a guess to change with the hours. But let her go? After what she has seen and heard? And knowing that you would be likely to tell her more? Women talk. They have tongues that you cannot still. It is a thing, you may be very sure, that he will not do."

Jiros rose with these words, as though the conversation had come to a good end, and did not look for a reply. He said: "I will come for you at the same hour as before," and so he went out.

Devereux saw that, if he had been sent by the Inca to test his truth, he would have been likely to press for a decisive reply. As it was, it would be understood that he would agree to that which the Inca proposed, and whether it were in sincerity, or with the intention of joining Jiros in flight, he had not been pressed to decide.

Well, it simplified what was next to be done, and appeared to postpone peril for a few hours, if not more.

While he debated this in his mind, two men entered, bringing his rifle, and other things of less account that were his, some of which he was glad to have.

Certainly, Jiros acted the part of a friend, and he was also clearly one who had power.

CHAPTER TWENTY-SEVEN

"ABOUT THE GIRL"

DEVEREUX was presented to the Inca for the third time, and in the same manner as before. To the question of whether he would undertake the offered mission he replied that he had considered it during the night, and thought that, if sufficient discretion were used, there was no reason that it should not succeed. He gave arguments for this view, as he had thought them out during the night, at which the Inca was pleased, being now satisfied that he had not only found one who would undertake what was required, but who had wit to succeed. Yet he did not intend to risk more than he need, and when Jiros summed his own dangers, there was one, for all subtlety, that he did not guess.

He knew that the Inca took drugs of a magic kind, by which he could see that which went on in a part of the earth, which was less surprising to him than it would be to those of Europe who know only of the unstable dreams that opium brings, and what cocaine can do in its single use. Jiros knew far more of the magic of potent drugs, and he knew that the Inca had a secret that took him further than was frequent with lesser men. What he did not know was that it would permit him at times to see into the minds of men, and ravish their private thoughts, so that his plans moved in the shadow of a danger they did not know.

Now the Inca, well-content with what he had heard, chose to clear the ground beyond doubt of a smaller thing. He said: "There is one matter on which he has my orders that he must not be the first to speak, but on which I would be clear beyond doubt. That is, that he has no lust for the girl who joined him upon the way, for whom I have a purpose in mind."

"I am assured of that," Jiros replied, "having spoken to him before we came, but I will ask him again."

He turned to Devereux to say: "The Inca has asked whether you are inclined to make further trouble about the girl, concerning whom he recalls that he had to forbid you to speak before. I would warn you to be cautious, not only of what you would have me say, but of how you look. I have told him, as it was most needful to do, that there will be no trouble concerning her, but you understand, between ourselves, that we will get her away."

"Very well. If that is agreed, I must trust your discretion for what you say."

"So you are wise to do. And I will tell you this. You may expect to see her when you get back to your own room, for I knew that while we were engaged here would be a safe time for her to be moved."

Devereux looked pleased at this, as Jiros may have meant that he should. Jiros turned to the Inca to say: "She was a woman he did not seek. I have made it clear that she must be nothing to him. But I have said more than the need required. It is on the treasure his heart is set."

The Inca said it was well. He added: "Tomorrow the Lord Carsholt will attend us in the Audience Hall, being more richly arrayed than he is now. And in four days you will have all arranged that he may be ready to start…. Let Kito know that I will have her with me tonight."

Jiros led Devereux back far enough for him to be in no doubt of the way to his own room, and then stayed. "You will not go wrong now," he said, "it being but one turn on the left ahead, and you may know that you will be undisturbed for the next hour, after which I must send to fetch her away."

CHAPTER TWENTY-EIGHT

JUANITA COMES

DEVEREUX exclaimed: "You are well? They have served you well?" and she spoke in almost the same words, asking before attempting reply.

They were glad to meet, as their voices showed but there was a constraint between them at first, which may have sprung in part from the strange clothes that they had been given to wear, making them half strangers to one another, beside that they were clear of the disorders of wilderness ways, so that he would hardly have known her for the girl from whom he parted three days before, had they come together in the midst of a crowded place.

"They have treated me well," she said, "but oh, it is a horrible den! I began to doubt that I should ever see you again."

He became aware of the language in which she spoke. "I did not know that you could speak English," he said, "till I heard you say a few words on the day when we came here."

"Well, I can. Don't you think it is prudent here to use a language which is not known?"

"I believe only Jiros speaks Portuguese."

"It is he I meant. He is one whom I cannot trust, though he has been friendly to me."

"And to me also. We must hope we are wrong, for it is on him that our lives depend.... You speak English well. Why did you not tell me before?"

"Why should I? I speak French also, but what that? Did you think I was born in that Indian lodge?

He heard the bitterness in her voice. "I should have been a fool," he replied, "if I had. But if they have treated you well, why do you call it a horrible den?"

"Because that is what it is. There are the screams in the night. I suppose you have heard what they are from? Well, no matter. There are worse things. I don't say the people are wholly bad. They are quite civilised in most of their ways, and good-mannered among themselves, and they seem gentle enough.... But there is a Soquito slave-girl, Kito, one of the Inca's favourites here, with whom I have been able to talk."

"But you wouldn't say that the Soquito ways are better than these?"

"I don't know that I mightn't even say that. The Soquitos eat their enemies, but this girl is the Inca's pet, and he will kill her in a few days from now more likely than not, and she will be eaten at a feast they hold to worship the sun."

"You mean they are cannibals, as the Aztecs were?"

"I oughtn't to say more than I know. She says it is only once a year—one sacrifice once a year—and the Inca is also Priest of the Sun, and kills them with his own hand. If I understand rightly, they are always favourite girls he has had, and they are expected to feel honoured rather than to object!"

Well, he looks rather a loathsome beast. I could believe that he would be equal to that. I don't know that I'm not rather pleased. It seems to give me more excuse for letting him down on a bargain we've just made, though I think I'd got plenty, without that.

"But I'm not sure that you should condemn the whole crowd. Cannibalism appears to have been general over the whole continent before Columbus turned up, except among the Red Indians, and their scalping and slow-torturing ways were a lot worse for the poor wretches they caught. And you know the Aztecs used to kill thousands at their religious feasts. If they've boiled it down to one annual victim here—"

She showed response to the buoyancy of his mood as she interrupted with an unseemly flippancy to object: "I believe they're roasted, not boiled."

"You know I didn't mean that. Your English seems to be as good as though you'd been born on the spot.... But we mustn't lose time chattering about nothing like this. I've got too much to explain."

160

He went on to tell her his own experiences while they had been kept apart, and as he did so her heart lightened to his own mood, for she saw, unexpressed but implicit in all he said, that it was for her safety that he had bargained and watched, and at last committed himself to this blind hazard of flight under the direction of one who must be a traitor to the monarch he served, and the race to which he belonged unless he were so to them.

In the hour that seemed so short before Jiros came with some haste of manner to lead her away, they had gained a greater intimacy, and one that seemed on another plane from all that had been during their long solitudes upon the river, and the harder journey across the land. It was as when men rise to resume life after a long illness has drawn them aside, and the familiar things have the freshness of a new world.

Devereux, left alone, recalled how he had resented her presence being thrust upon him at first, how he had stubbornly resolved that he would be caught in no entanglement that he could not break, how he had held aloof in the long hot solitudes of the night, as some might ridicule that he had preferred, and some would wonder that he had been able to do. If the time could again be his, he thought that he would use it in better ways, though it was not clear to himself what he regretted of opportunities lost, or of what reticences he might still be glad.

If he could be sure that these opportunities might not be forever lost…! In the evening Jiros came to discuss plans in more detail than he had attempted before.

Chapter Twenty-Nine

A Plan of Flight

KITO came to the Inca's bed, as she was always willing to do. She supposed that it might be the last time, which she expected to learn, about which she trembled at times; but it was not the way of her race to lose present pleasure for the prospect of future pain. She knew that what would be, would, which she was powerless to change. She would not be tempted to kick at the goad's pricks, and she would therefore have less trouble than do those who struggle to push evil away with desperate, impotent hands.

The Inca played with her till the mood passed, letting her doubt for that time. It pleased his habit of power to feel that she waited in terror, even while she was thrilled in another way, to learn whether he had decided to let her live, or to die at his hands in the coming week.

"Well," he said at last, "you can go now. But tell me first of what sort is the white girl who was for some time in the lodge of your own tribe. Have you spoken with her...? Is she well-formed and unblemished enough lo be fit for the Holy Altar of the Father of Light?"

Kito looked a moment's relief, but after that appeared to be rather sullen than glad. "She is well enough. She is well enough for a white girl."

Her tone conveyed that a girl with a white skin could not deserve more than measured praise. She added: "She is a virgin, more likely than not. I suppose you know that."

Having said that, she had a fear that she might have spoken her own doom, which she did not wish, although jealousy might be a strong urge. She was afraid of pain, and most reluctant to die, but—

to have her throat pierced by the Inca's knife, in the awed sight of a hundred thousand, women and men—to be carved that night on the Inca's board—they were honour that any girl might wish to delay, but that none would be content to finally miss!

But the Inca answered easily, as concerning that he already knew. "Is it so? Well, it can be mended by then. I think you must rein desire for a year's time, when you shall come to the most excellent end that a woman may."

He watched her go with a wish that he might try the drugs again, for there was much now that it was vital that he should learn, but his hand shook, and his eyes had that difficulty in focusing which he was beginning to dread. He must defer it for two nights, or perhaps three. There would still be time. For this night he would be glad to sleep in a natural way.

So he went to such rest as will come to those whose nerves are shattered by self-abuse, and meanwhile Jiros sat in Devereux's room, and expounded his plans.

"I will advise the Inca," he said, "that there is no occasion to send you with a load of treasure, and that burdened mules would be hard to get over the Peruvian border without that which they bore being examined, which must not be risked. Treasure in bulk should not be sent until you have made arrangement for its transit, and for its reception in other lands. He will see the reason for that, and if you talk in the same way, using all the knowledge you have (which may be greater than mine), he will agree that you shall first take no more than a bag of well-chosen gems, which will be a fortune more than enough, the stones being what you have seen.

"We will arrange for you to start at the dawn, the escort being assembled on the mainland the night before, but in fact we will leave here as soon as midnight is past, and rouse them with a tale that we have the Inca's orders to proceed earlier so that none may see where we go.

"And as to how we shall get away without fear that we may be stayed by the guards, I will make no secret of that. There is a flooded passage (as you are unlikely to know), which goes under the lake, and is filled from a sluice which can be closed, after which the water it contains will be drained into a great pit, the same lever which closes out the lake opening the way to the drain. We shall come out in the forest edge, which is not the way we should go, but it is a circuit which will not be too lengthy to make, and there is no other way of escape that can be so secret and sure.

"And when we are once away, being unburdened, and having the best beasts that the land contains (you may trust that I shall not leave that in doubt we shall not be easy to overtake."

Devereux listened to a plan that sounded good in itself, and that increased his confidence in the man by whom it was proposed, because he had seen the exit to the passage, of which Jiros could not be aware.

"It sounds," he said, "a good plan. But could we not proceed in an even less hazardous way? Why should I not start openly, as the Inca will expect me to do, and you could come to the place where the escort will be awaiting for us to mount, as having the office to see that I am well started upon the way, and there would be no more to be done at last than to tell a man to get down from his mule, and you will mount, and we ride away?"

Devereux saw the flaw in this plan before the sentence was done, but having asked, he let Jiros reply.

"We can do that, if you will abandon the girl; and though we should have the risk of instant pursuit, I do not think that it would be more than a small chance, for there would be none to question till it should come to the Inca's knowledge that I had not returned. Yes, if you will let the girl go, I should call it the safer way, but it was that which I though you would be unwilling to do."

"You were right in that. But are you so sure that the Inca will not consent that I take her, now that all else is agreed? After all, she can be nothing to him, and he may wish me to be content."

"It would be useless to ask, for the reason I have given before. He would consider that women talk, and he has been twice told that she is of no value to you. If we should go to him now with another tale, not only would suspicion wake but he would see a new cause that she should not go, as she would become a hostage for your return.

"And, beside that, he has a purpose, as I have reason to think, to make her of use in another way. For we are now within a few days of the great Festival of the Sun, at which it has been the custom for as long a time as we have been here, to sacrifice a girl who has first been in the Inca's bed, that our God may lead us back to our own land. It is plain to see that if a white girl has been found for this for the first time in four hundred years, it will both please our Father the

164

Sun, and will be a symbol to all of the overthrow of her race in the coming war."

Devereux did not like this, either in itself or in the way in which Jiros spoke, which was as though he himself were a worshipper at the Sun-god's shrine, as he might be expected to be. If that were so—He asked abruptly: "Do you believe that?"

Jiros looked at him with a smile that was hard to read. "Who knows? The Inca sent me to Rio for three years that I might learn the tongue in which we now speak. I learned other things. But if you escape with the girl the question will not arise."

Jiros went, leaving Devereux to his own thoughts, among which was one that he did not like.

He thought the plan itself to be simple and good, and one concerning which no suspicion should be aroused. For why should he desire to escape underground during the night, when he would be free to go on the next day. So long as the Inca did not suspect that Juanita was of value to him, he would see no reason to suspect that which it would be a mere folly to try.

But when he thought of Juanita herself, and the perils in which she lay, he had a sharp dread, and a moment's doubt of whether he were not doing a wrong to her, whose safety he would have put before all, as it had seemed to him that in fact he did.

For he saw that, if he had been frank as to her value at first, and also sincere in his promise to do which the Inca asked, she might have had no worse than detention to fear, and even that might soon have been overcome, whereas now the horror which Kito had confided to her, was to sit itself down at her own door.

Could he change his plans now, even at the last hour? He did not see that he could, so that the temptation, whether it would have been strong or weak, did not arise. There was the impregnable fact (as he thought, but overlooking one thing), that he could communicate nothing to the Inca but through the mouth of Jiros, and it was certain that Jiros would help him, if at all, in his own way.

No. They must go on as they had planned to do. But he saw that the stakes grew higher at every throw.

Chapter Thirty

The Audience Hall

SO far, Devereux had seen a vast treasure, which had been accumulated in ancient times by men who were long dead, and whose children had been scattered and overthrown.

He had met the owner of this incredible wealth, a man formidable or dignified rather in his position than in himself, in a small room, and conversed with him through an interpreter, who, whatever else he might be, was, on his own word, a disloyal rogue.

There had been talk of a nation, and of projects to shake the world, but words are easy to say, and visual evidence, apart from the treasure itself, had not largely appeared.

He knew that he was in an island fortress, built of most massive stones, which he had entered by such a water-gate as could only be passed by a small boat, and that since then he had seen long passages, and various rooms of no great height or size, and perhaps two score of armed men, or attendants of different grades. It left to imagination a large and most doubtful field.

It may have been to give Devereux another view of his rule, and to realise that what he had so far seen was no more than his private rooms, that the Inca ordered that he should be present in the Hall of Audience on the next day, being an occasion when he would deal justice to those who made appeal to him from the lower courts.

Devereux found himself placed in a position of some apparent honour, on a high dais, where he was seated among some scores of those who appeared to be the principal officers of a court with which he had not previously come into contact. The Hall itself was lofty and dignified in a bare way, its austerity being relieved by mural

166

paintings somewhat Egyptian in their effects, though of a distinction that it was easy to see.

There were no women among the groups of the Inca's officials, nor among the public assembly in the body of the Hall, excepting a few who were there as witnesses or parties to the cases which would be heard. But there was a group in a screened place at the side of the Hall, so arranged that they were invisible to the general public below, among whom Devereux was able to recognise Juanita, garlanded with flowers and freshly attired. Kito, in a tunic brightly sashed, very different from the nudity of her own sombre forest-youth, was at her side, and able to tell her something of what went on, as far as it was understood by her own quick wits, and the thin bridge of a primitive language, imperfectly learned, allowed the transit of thought.

The whole scene, apart from the austerity of the Hall itself, was one of colour and light. Feathered headdresses were emphatic in their brilliant contrasting colours: gold armlets and anklets gleamed. The Inca, below the imperial black-and-white, wore a circlet of blue, from which descended a scarlet fringe. His white tunic was edged with scarlet. His arms shone with jewels. A priceless necklace was round his throat. Scarlet and blue were the feathered ornaments on his knees. His throne was an unearthly dragon of jewelled gold, its fanged, gaping mouth forming the canopy over his head.

The Council of Four, who sat slightly below him on either hand, were as gaily attired, though their ornaments might be of a less costly kind. Devereux had occasion to see the truth of the Inca's words, that Brazilian feathers are brighter than precious stones.

Jiros came to Devereux's side, to interpret the cases and the justice the Inca dealt. They were all final appeals from decisions of mainland courts, where there could be no doubt that there was a great population beyond the lake, as highly civilised as that which the Spaniards found when they made Cuzco their spoil.

The roof of the Hall was gapped in such a way that a sunbeam would be narrow and bright across some part of the middle floor during the three hours that the court sat; and as the proceedings commenced a goblet of some royal drink was ceremonially bathed in this band of light, and offered to the Inca's lips, while the audience prostrated themselves, either to the Sun or to Him—a distinction which may not have been clear to their own minds.

Afterwards, each appealing criminal, and each witness called, would kneel to kiss the sunbeam before giving evidence which must be that which the Light required.

As to the justice the Inca dealt, it was hard for Devereux to appraise, only hearing the cases through the summaries which Jiros gave, but some of them had a sensible sound.

A usurer was to be hanged till he was half dead and let go with the knowledge that, if he should offed again, he would have a longer time on the rope.

A man who had stolen through poverty had his appeal allowed, but the head official of his district was to be flogged for the inefficiency which caused such poverty to occur. A gossip-spreader was to be hanged by the feet till he was dead.

"Which is," Jiros observed, "a wise and most ancient law."

CHAPTER THIRTY-ONE

JUANITA HEARS KITO'S VIEWS

"THERE will be perhaps fifty miles to cross of our own land, which is tilled and fertile, and scattered with the dwellings of men," Jiros explained, "and after that there will be three or four hundred more of a barren and desert plain, where the heat is great, and there will be no water at this time of the year, and then the montana belt, which is a land of mountain-gorges—forest, valley, and height— very hard to cross, but having water and food, and where we shall come at last to the roofs of men, and after that there will he the Andes to climb, by which way we shall be at Lima at last."

"It may be a better way than we came," Devereux allowed, "but it has a poor sound."

"It is much better than that, which it is a marvel that you endured."

"How soon are we to start?"

"On the third morning from now. The treasure will be opened on the previous day, and the chosen jewels given to your own hand. But we shall have a guard whom you will have no reason to fear. For indeed, to our people's minds, the jewels are pretty gauds, but of less worth than a well-built hut, or a fruitful tree."

"Well, that may be comfort to know, and it will be an advantage that you will be there, for I should speak no word of their tongue, nor, I suppose, would they mine."

"Much can be done by signs, if there be patience and a good will."

"It is what I would believe without test. Does Juanita know when we shall start?"

"I will let her know in sufficient time."

"When can I see her again?"

"Not while we are here. It would be a most foolish risk. You are secure while you show that you care nothing for her."

"To see her would be no crime. Need the Inca know?"

"It is most likely he would. Kito talks. She is with Juanita much, who can speak her tongue."

"Could she not be told to be quiet?"

"That would be the maddest of all. Kito is the Inca's woman."

"Being a slave, and perhaps to be killed by him?"

"It may seem a wonder to you, but she would look on it another way."

"It is a thing hard to believe."

"Can you not wait for three days? What is it that you are so anxious to say?"

"Nothing that cannot be said through you. I am a fool. I admit that. I am impatient to get away, and the time is slow."

He saw that to press for another interview with Juanita would be folly, there being risks enough without that, but he was restless with a premonition of evil which may have had no more foundation than the danger in which they stood, and the fact that he must be idle to await an event that was slow to come. But great as his disquiet might be, it would have been more if he could have heard the instructions that the Inca gave Kito at the same hour.

The Inca had sent for Kito, to her surprise, which had been a close neighbour to fear, for it was not his custom to have her again so soon, nor was she one for whom he would be likely to send, except for one purpose alone. He had told her that she was to live for another year, but could be content that she would be honoured after that time. She had realised, after hearing this, that it was an event that she would be pleased to defer. Had he changed again? Having seen the knife recede from her throat, she did not want it to hurry back. She went with the submissive smile which he would expect her to show, but as she knelt to him, and her head bent to the ground, which was the first greeting she had to give, she shook like a light bough in the wind.

The Inca took no notice of that. He said: "Kito, you can talk the language of the white girl?"

"No, but she can talk mine, having lived with a tribe of our language for many months."

"That is the same thing. Have you told her the use for which she has been brought here by the Sun's will?"

"No. I have told her nothing of that."

"Then you will say no more now than that I shall require her here within three nights, for which honour she must be await in a ready way. For that, you tell her all she should know, which you are able to do. And when the word comes you will guide her here, but you do not know which night it will be."

"Lord, so I will. Shall I tell her also that she will be sacrificed in the next week?"

"You shall tell her that in good time, but not now."

"Lord, I hear."

Kito went, and the Inca turned his mind to matters of more account, knowing that that would be done, for Kito was of an obedience he could not doubt.

Kito told Juanita that she would be required in the Inca's bed within the three next nights, never doubting that she would be glad, for what higher honour could she desire?

Juanita had been told already by Jiros that they could not attempt escape before the third night, or the fourth, because neither would the escort be ready nor the jewels have been released. She saw a trap open before her feet which it might be hard to avoid, and her blood paused in her heart with a sinking fear, for she was one who loved both honour and life, and she saw that they might be one more than she would be able to keep.

She looked at Kito, and remembered other things she had told her before, with a sharp doubt. "That is not all," she said, "there is more."

Kito was not a good liar. "It is all I was told to say."

"You have said enough."

She became silent. It was a matter on which she had wit to see that she could not call Kito her friend. Should she let Devereux know? She had a well-founded fear that he would be stirred to precipitate the event in some dangerous way. She did not want that. It would be likely to bring them all to a quick end. She wanted honour—and life.

Should she confide in Jiros? She saw it for the folly it would be likely to prove. They trusted Jiros because they must. If he should not betray, it must be because his plans walked with theirs. What he would do if he should see a new risk for himself would be hard to

171

guess, but she was sure that he would not consider her, except as a pawn in his own game.

Neither, she rightly supposed, would he understand her at all. Why should she object so much to an hour in the Inca's bed? She might choose it, or not. But this was a moment of greater doubts. They faced issues of fortune, and life and death. They had to keep the Inca unsuspecting and quiet, and if she could help to do that, it should be done without fuss. She must fight in a woman's way.

As to telling Devereux, if it should be with the object of making trouble, or likely to have that result, he would be sure to refuse. It was the one point on which they would be more or less of one mind. She doubted that she could persuade him to the prudence which she saw to be the one small chance that she had, especially as she had no plan of what she should do, but only to delay to the last, and to trust her wit.

She had a fear of another kind that he might misread, or even despise what her heart held. She knew with an instinct bitter and sure that he had a vague hate of the experiences through which she had gone while in the Soquitos' hands, of which she would never speak. It was a feeling that stronger forces had overcome, but it was still there.

If she should tell him that she was in danger of dishonour at the Inca's hands, and should add: "But there is nothing that you can do. It is a risk we must take. You must leave me to deal with it as best I can. Fly at once? It would be a most hopeless attempt. It would be our deaths," might he not misread her as one whose honour was content with a low seat? Might it not be to lose his love, as the price at which she strove to save both his life and hers in what after all, might be no more than a lost game?

No, she must fight this alone, for with allies it would be a battle already lost. And she had wit for weapon—and a revolver beside, in which five cartridges were still good.

She considered that if she were alone with the Inca (as she imagined that it would be) he should be easy to kill. But after that the programme became obscure. She could not imagine that they would be allowed to go without it being noticed that he was dead, nor that Jiros would join such a flight unless the treasure were already in Devereux's hands. She could not tell what he would do if she should tell him that the Inca was dead, but she was sure that he would think only of his own skin, and she felt sure that his thoughts would not be healthy for her.

Besides, how would she ever find him to tell? She would have no words with which to enquire, even if those she might meet as she wandered about in the night (as she supposed it would be) would be obedient to do her will. It was probable that she would not see Jiros at all before there would be discovery of the Inca's death.

She might find Devereux's room, having been there once, though she was doubtful of that. But what use would it be, except to involve him in her own fate? She saw that the Inca's death might be a poor end for those with whose lives she was more concerned.

Then might she not threaten that which she did not do? Even Incas are mortal, and, like other mortals, object to die. It was an idea which was well enough if its details were left obscure, but it became foolish at a near view.

If she could have talked, there would have been a more feasible chance. But was she to flourish a weapon the use of which he might not understand, and make treaty for her own honour and his life in a pantomime of action without words? It was absurd.

There was always this curse, that she could not talk to him, except through Jiros or Kito, and she sure that neither of them would help her or understand.

Seeking a better idea, it occurred to her that a diplomatic illness might cut the knot. She sounded Kito on that, the girl having opened the subject first, according to the orders she had.

Kito said: "I am to tell you how you shall behave when the Inca shall send for you, so that you will give him all the pleasure you can. There is much that you will have been taught during the months that you were in the Soquito lodge, for in some ways our customs are like to those that these people have, and what men would have us do may be the same in all lands, but there are some things you should know."

"Never mind about them," Juanita replied, "I heard enough before now, as you say. Besides there is time enough. For the next four days, or perhaps five, I shall not go. If the Inca should send, you will tell him I am not well."

Kito looked at her with puzzled, questioning eyes. "Do you think, when the Inca calls, you can send such an answer as that? And, besides, it is not true."

"It is true enough. I have a pain in my head that will not go. It might last for a week. It may be much worse than it is now."

"But the Inca will not care how your head feels. It is not concerned in what he will have you do. Besides, women do not delay when the Inca calls. *It is not done*."

Kito said the last words as though they must make Juanita see that it had been silly talk. Etiquette was more rigid here than in the civilisations of the Old World, and it had been more rigid still among the Soquitos, where she had been reared. To say "it is not done" was to silence dissent, unless it could be shown that the argument was untrue.

"But I am white," Juanita replied, "and in my land, if we are unwell, it is good reason to ask delay."

"Well," Kito replied, with reason upon her side, "you are somewhere else now. And I am here to tell you of any customs you do not know. When the Inca sends, you will find it best to go on your own legs, for if you delay you will find there are others that will move you along. And if you are dull when you arrive, I do not say he will care, but he may not have you again."

Kito stopped at the last words, being what she would not have said had she thought first, for she knew that Juanita would not be wanted a second time, be she warm or cold, so that they did not apply.

Juanita noticed that abruptness of pause, which she understood, so that it confirmed the fear she already had. She said: "What you mean is that he plans my death, as he does yours?" She had almost added: "If I should be here in a week's time," and checked herself with a quicker rein than Kito had been able to do, their confidences, which were frank enough within the limits that circumstances allowed, being held alike within watchful bounds.

"That," Kito replied, "is what I did not say."

"It was not said, it was thought."

Kito, whose limitations in lying have been observed already, did not deny this. She said: "Well, life is what we are in no hurry to lose, as I have found, who am to live for another year. But if you com to that end (which I tell you again that I have not said) you may consider how great an honour it is, and more especially for one who has a white skin (I do not mean to be rude. You could not help how you were born.) And that a hundred thousand people will see you die."

174

"It may be the fault of my skin," Juanita replied "but to me it would be no honour at all. Neither are you consistent in what you say, for are not men killed and eaten by your own tribe to do them the greatest insult you can? Do you not say that it is to make them of the level of beasts because they are killed for food?"

Kito was a good-tempered girl, but she made gesture of irritation as she replied: "When you say that, you confound opposite things, and you cannot think that I shall make patient reply. Are beasts for food killed by the Inca's hand? Are they sacrifice to the Sun, whose Godhead Itself regards us so much that for our blood He may give great blessings to men? When an enemy is slaughtered and cooked, do man thousands look on, making it a festival day?"

"All this may be," Juanita replied, seeing that the argument had become waste of words, "but it remains an honour I do not want."

"Yet," Kito persisted, "you should try to think of it in the right way, for none can change the customs that rule the world, and it is by right thinking that sorrow is put aside."

And seeing some wisdom in this (though it was not for her use), Juanita allowed Kito the last word.

CHAPTER THIRTY-TWO

CLIMAX FOR JUANITA

THE next two days were of a concealed tension on every side. It was understood that the escort was being assembled with a care suitable to the importance of the duty it would discharge, and the hardship of the journey it had to take.

Jiros took a willing care about this, for he saw that there would be heavy burden upon the mules, and that they must still be fit to outpace pursuit, which might not be more than a few hours behind. He had advocated that there should be many be many beasts light loads, saying that it would be safer thus, if some should falter and die in the desert, were they could not be replaced. He had a secret plan also to requisition others upon the way, so that their loads should not be more than that of a man, and they could keep pace with those that the escort rode.

Devereux observed him to be one who planned with scrupulous care, which gave a good hope that they would come clear. He appeared to be adroit at interpreting, also, at the long conferences the Inca held during these two days, or, if he did not interpret accurately, he must have been skilful in saying the right thing, for the Inca's confidence appeared to increase, both in Devereux himself, and in that which he was to be commissioned to do.

As he was questioned on these matters, and must give his mind to the details of what he was resolved that he would never attempt, he found it hard at times to talk in the right way, and at others he would find himself to be snared in his own plans, so that he would become half resolved to turn his sails to that course, and must remind himself of Juanita's peril, and of the evils of worldwide war, to ease his mind of the treachery of that which he purposed to do. Had he talked to the Inca direct, he might have found the deception too hard to sustain.

But it seemed that all went well till the second night, and it was only after Devereux had retired to his own room, so that he knew nothing of what occurred, that the Inca said to Jiros: "I will have the white woman tonight. Kito is to bring her in two hours from now. It is likely that I shall require Kito also to stay, so that she may interpret any orders that I may give."

Jiros was used both to think quickly, and to conceal thought. He did not care a straw what the Inca should do to Juanita, nor would he have said that it could matter over greatly to her. It was her business to get away with her throat whole, and to give less thought to a minor harm. Emphatically, it was her business to act so that she would not imperil those who were of more importance than any woman could be, that is to say Devereux and himself.

But he had lived in Rio for two years, and he knew that some white women are oversensitive on such points, to which he would have said that they attribute too great importance, both to avoid and to do. He saw possible trouble, and for the space of time that his eyelids flickered and rose he had debated whether he should propose a delay. But what excuse could he give which would not contradict statements already made? And if he should be overruled, and then trouble come, would he not, by his hesitation have drawn suspicion towards himself, as having had knowledge he had not disclosed, from which his reluctance came? He decided that it would be too dangerous to attempt.

He considered also that, though he had said that Devereux cared nothing for her, he had not committed himself as to her own feelings, or how she would now behave. There would be the less risk in letting the Inca do as he would, without protest from him. Let him rape her tonight, and if she should play the fool, it was she who would be most likely to pay, either with throat or back, and he a least would stand clear. Tomorrow? Well, he must see how it would be. He could still keep them apart. He could say that Juanita would come out by another way. In fact, the position would not present so much difficulty to his own plans as to those which Devereux supposed him to have.

So, with no more than a second's pause, he answered that she should be sent, treating it in the casual tone that it required, and the Inca let him go, saying no more.

But the Inca had noticed that second's pause, that moment's flicker of eyes, and in his mind a small seed of suspicion grew, where he had not been trusting of choice before, but because Jiros was the one man who could speak a language which the Englishman understood.

He would not have gone so far as he had, had he not planned to put the loyalty of him to whom he would trust so much to a sure test on the next night. Now he hesitated as to whether it would not be better to reverse the order of what he did. Let the girl wait. He would take a large dose of the drug while his hand was firm and his mind clear. He would explore Jiros's thoughts to the last lurking, half-formed design, and after that he would know what to do...

But he put the idea by. After all, there would be time enough on the next night, and there was more pleasure in this. He was always disposed to put off the use of that magic mixture of drugs to the last moment he could. He could not forget how ill he would feel on the next day. He would ask Kito one or two questions, and, for the moment, be guided by her replies.

Juanita took the summons in a way that gave Kito no clue to her thoughts, which she would have found it hard to translate into meaning words. She knew the crisis had come, but could not tell how she would act, even now. She found means to attach her weapon beneath the single garment she wore, and took what comfort she could from that. She wished Devereux were at her side, but she had the sense to see that she would be little better for that.

She had never seen that it could be either honour or pleasure to die by the Inca's hand, but she felt that she might be conscious of both if she should come to put a bullet between his ribs. She felt that it could not be in a better place. But how could it be safely done? Not certainly while Kito was at her side. Unless she should kill Kito too, and that she could see that she never would.

She had changed much in the last two years, since she had left an environment of girlhood that even Devereux did not guess. Or perhaps it should be said that circumstances changing around her had shown her more thoroughly to herself than she would otherwise have been able to see. She could kill the Inca with a firm hand, and it would be a pleasure to do. But to kill a girl who had no quarrel with her? Not for life, nor honour, could she do that, for what honour would there be left when the bullet struck...? She heard Kito say: "But you cannot go in those flowers! They have been worn since before noon. Do you not know what decency is?" She let Kito do as she would, though she thought the flowers to be as fresh as the occasion required....

The Inca looked at Juanita, and she at him. She had the eyes of a frightened deer, but her lips were set in a hard line. He was not concerned as to how she looked, neither was he surprised. He had explored her mind in the night, and he knew to whom she would have preferred to go. There was something else that it was important to learn. He had thought of a question the answer to which might be nothing or very much. He asked Kito: "When did she last have speech with the Englishman?

Kito meant Juanita no harm. She meant harm to none. But to lie to the Inca would have been beyond the range of her wildest dream. She said: "Not since she went to his room, it was, I think, two days ago."

"Being led by whom?"

"By the lord Jiros."

"And how long was she there?"

"He brought her back in two hours, or perhaps less. I was not careful to know."

"Take her back. I have changed my mind for this night."

Juanita stood listening to words she could not comprehend, and wondering how loud a shot would sound in that room of stone. Would he be easy to kill? Would he understand what she had done? She hoped he would not die too quickly for that. She felt a fierce hate constricting her throat, which came from fear of her own end, which she supposed might not be much longer delayed, and might be of a worse kind.

She saw the Inca give an abrupt jerk of his hand, as though he threw both her and Kito aside. He spoke again in a vexed way. He had said: "Take her back. Is it not clear? I have changed my mind for this night." Kito translated that.

Juanita gave a short laugh. Would the dream break? Kito pulled her away.

CHAPTER THIRTY-THREE

THE WATER THAT OTHERS DRINK

IT may be thought that if the Inca had decided to explore Devereux's mind, he would have learned more than he did, by a shorter way. But there were four reasons against that, and all good.

The first is that it was against Jiros that his suspicion was turned, for he supposed (and had been near to proof) that he was a traitor before.

The second is that, as Jiros was at the centre of all, being translator to those who could not talk excepting through him, he must know most, not only of his own mind, but of those among whom he moved.

And the third, which may have been most potent of all in deciding the Inca as to whom he should test, was that men think half in pictures and half in words, and Devereux's words would have no meaning for him. It was a difficulty which had limited his exploration of Juanita's mind, though in that case he had learnt enough, seeking as he did for mere emotion rather than that which the intellect weighs and plans; but he was set now on a harder search.

The last reason was that it was Jiros who had been on his mind, and upon whom he could best concentrate all his thoughts, as it was needful to do if his drugged spirit were not to wander about in a vague way, collecting facts which might be of no value to him. It was under this compulsion that he had sent Juanita away, lest she should intrude too far to confuse his mind, for otherwise he might have taken any pleasure that she could give, and still have had as much of the night left as his purpose asked.

So he went to his drugged sleep, and when it was done, and he rose at a late hour, his head ached, and his hand shook, as he had known that it would be, but apart from that he was a sombre and thoughtful man.

He had learnt some things that were simple and clear, and some that were less easy to understand, but none that it was pleasant to know.

He had learnt the truth of the plan that Jiros had formed, which was very much what Devereux had understood it to be, with the difference that Devereux was to die in a way which, to the Inca, was easy to understand.

The part that was not clear was the extent to which Devereux might be accomplice or dupe, or the mere victim of a plot with which he had nothing to do.

This obscurity came from the fact that Jiros, having shown Devereux as much of his plan as needful to make him its willing tool, had put it, in that form, out of his mind, which had brooded rather upon that which he meant it to take. And the conversations which he had translated between the Inca and Devereux had been rendered truly enough, for Devereux, whatever he might have thought, had talked as though he would fulfil the Inca's designs, so that Jiros's mind was a warehouse of two freights—his own plot, which would betray the Inca and Devereux alike, and the plans of which they two had talked, which had passed backward and forward across his tongue, and which it had been necessary for him to apprehend in an intelligent manner.

There was one other feature of his design which gave the Inca some puzzled thought. It had been clear that Jiros considered Juanita as part of the spoil that he would bear away, not, as the Inca had understood, as having any such bargain with her, but by the easy rule of which his sojourn in Rio had done nothing to cleanse his mind, that where the wealth goes there the woman will.

He would (so he had planned) have a great wealth, and Juanita in his power for the long journey he had to take, and an escort who would be obedient in all, believing that they were doing the Inca's will. If he could not bring her to his feet in that time, either by force or bribe, she having no other shelter in which to trust—well, she would be unlike most of her sex, and he would be a surprised man!

That was clear. But how would Juanita become part of that fleeing caravan, when, as Jiros knew, the Inca had destined her for a different fate? He could not discover this, there being no more in Jiros's present thoughts than assumption that she would be there.

181

It was this point that puzzled him more than all, and caused him to doubt Devereux's faith; yet he was acute to observe that neither he nor Juanita could have heard anything except through Jiros's mouth, and to judge them, whatever they might have said or agreed, was a vain task unless it were first known what had been said to them.

If he should dispose of Jiros in a suitable manner (as he was now resolved), could he communicate with them in another way, or would it be necessary to assume Devereux's guilt and to deal with him as guilt deserved putting an end, for the time, to a broken dream?

He pondered this, and considered that in Kito there was a possible means of communicating with Devereux. Poor and indirect, but it was the only one that remained.

He could talk to Kito in his own tongue. She could translate to Juanita in the Soquito language, which Juanita had learnt, and Juanita could translate again to Devereux in Portuguese. It had the difficulty that it is not everything that can be said in the Soquito tongue, and still less in those words of it that Juanita would be likely to know. It had the advantage that Kito could be trusted in what she said.

Having resolved this in his mind, he decided that matters should go on for that day much as they would have done had he left Jiros's mind to itself during the night.

In the afternoon he had the treasure vaults opened again, and he allowed Devereux (Jiros giving some willing help) to select stones enough to fill a small sack, of which no inventory was taken, and indeed, it would have seemed foolish to do, for by the side of those that remained they were just nothing at all. But, at the Inca's own direction, he chose them with care that he might have the least weight for the best value he could, and some of all varieties of precious gems that were there, for it was certain that it would be easier to dispose of three great stones of each of a dozen kinds than of three dozen of one.

The total number he took was, of course, much greater than that, and he would have been content to stop earlier than he did, but this he feared to propose in view of the magnitude of the operations which he was expected to undertake. In the end, he had about sixty pounds' weight of diamonds and other gems of quality which would not be easy to match if all the world's markets from Amsterdam to New York should be searched, and their hidden treasures laid bare.

"For this night," the Inca said, giving the words to Jiros to be conveyed in the customary manner, "you shall have these in your own charge, and (though I do not say there is need) there shall be a guard at your door, and tomorrow you shall set out at the noon hour, after one or two matters have been put in order before you go."

Jiros translated this. He added: "You need not be concerned for the guard, who will take their orders from me. Before morning we shall be gone."

He spoke with assurance, knowing that none around would be able to understand, and being so near to success that he had become confident that all would go smoothly now.

He had some anxiety in the earlier day as to what might have occurred in the night between the Inca and Juanita, and her reaction thereto. But he had visited her quarters during the morning, ostensibly to warn her of the plans which had been made for the coming flight, and he found her unruffled of mood, by which he judged that she had taken it in a sensible way.

Now he waited but a short time, and went boldly to visit Devereux, seeing that it would not be an unnatural thing for him to do, as being concerned that all should be in order for the next day. But what he said was this: "In three hours from now the guard will have orders that they need not longer remain, as all is stilled for the night. So when you have allowed them time to draw entirely away, you will go yourself, bearing the bag, and what else you will. You will turn twice to the left, and then go on until you come to an opening on the right hand which will lead you, within a few yards, to a flight of stone steps, down which you will go, counting thirty, and when you stand on the thirtieth step, you will be able to feel a metal lever set in a recess in the wall which you will pull hard to the right. You will find that it will not be easy to hold, but if you persist it will slacken after a time, and remain there of itself.

"You will then go down thirty steps more, and will come to another lever, which you will serve in the same way. And after that you will go down a thirty steps that remain, till you come to the water's brink, where you must stay until you hear the gurgling of the water as it recedes, which should be in not more than an hour's time, if the levers have been properly pulled, and in an hour's time after that the passage should be free of water from end to end."

Devereux did not like this overmuch. He saw that there would be two hours, if not three, during which he could not escape, and he would be exposed to discovery during that time in a helpless way. But he could not say that he knew of a better plan.

"You might repeat that," he said, "till I know it well."

When he was sure that he had it right, he asked "And when may I expect Juanita and you?"

"I will bring her in time enough. But it is to get her forth from the women's quarters that is the hardest part, which I take myself, it being that which you could not do. But if there should be alarm when I do that, we shall wish the passage to have become dry, and it will be more risk for all if I bring her before I should."

He added: "I might get another to pull the levers while you lie still, but it is an added risk to make a confidant now; and I may tell you, for your content, that the passages go through a part of the castle which is deserted during the night, and that is why I lodged you here at the first, for I looked ahead."

"So I see that you do. Will there be light all the way?"

"The lamps in the passages always burn. The steps will be dark. You will take your lamp from this room."

"I have no more than two hands! I will do what I must. I will hope to see you again in the night."

Jiros went, saying no more. Devereux thought he would rest while he could, for he supposed his chance for that would be soon done, but he was to find that it had not come. He was disturbed almost at once by a sound of voices and feet, and a sight of the guard falling with faces forward upon the floor, for the Inca entered, having his feathered crest on his head, and with Juanita and Kito coming behind.

Juanita spoke in English. She said: "Listen to what I say, but do not allow surprise to appear. The Inca wants me first to explain that he is anxious to reassure himself that his plans are well understood. He says that he has had to depend on Jiros entirely, who may not have translated everything as he should, and he would like to check this by confirming the plans you have made, through Kito and me.

"I suppose the Inca to have become suspicious of Jiros, if not of you, but you may be able to answer in ways that will reassure his doubt."

"Yes, I may do that."

"But there is more. Whether or not the Inca suspect that Jiros is false to him, there is good cause to think that he is meaning treason to you. I must not talk too long now, but among the questions I ask I will tell you more."

The examination that followed was slow, for Kito found it hard to understand much that the Inca asked, and far harder to convey it to Juanita in the Soquito tongue, but its tendency was to relieve suspicion in the Inca's mind as far as Devereux was concerned, for he judged correctly that all the three were endeavouring to elucidate that which he was anxious to know, which there was, indeed, no cause to avoid.

But he could not prevent nor observe that Juanita should interpose other things in the strange language she spoke, and so she said, not at once, but among much which it would be tiresome to reproduce: "It is from Kito I have the tale, and you may take it for true. She has a brother, Gobana, who is employed in bringing provisions and other things from the mainland here. There is a river in this country—or it may be a pond or spring, it is no matter for that, and she did not say—but there is a water here which the people may safely drink, being in some way immune, but if a stranger taste it he will die of a fever that none can cure.

"Yesterday, Gobana was employed to bring Jiros this water in a full gourd, which he did, it being his part to obey, and what matter was it to him, so Kito says, or how should he know for what use it would be required?

"But he told Kito this in an idle way, and she thought it must be intended for us, one or both, for we are the strangers here.

"She was troubled by this, for she does not think it to be done by the Inca's will, but if she should make it known, her brother, having no proof, may be disbelieved and soon dead; or if it were required for some innocent use, he might be punished as one having a loose and dangerous tongue. So she decided to warn me of what she knew, on the bargain that we should not reveal that she had spoken at all."

"I should say it is true," Devereux replied, "for it is a trap into which Peixoto fell, and, it may be, by which he died. For his warning to those who should come here was to avoid water which others drank, which has not been simple to understand. If we get clear tonight, it will be his purpose to destroy me, if not you also, and to take the jewels without being burdened by us."

185

"It would be a silly thing, there being plenty for both."

"So it would. But we know that greed has a large mouth, and he may not understand how vast is the wealth we shall bear away—if ever we go."

"Well, we may be able to deal with this, having been warned."

"Yes. The girl is a good friend. But we have troubles enough without this. I wish we could go by ourselves, and the way we came, even though we might lack things we shall have."

"Yes. But we cannot alter the plan now. It is too late."

Devereux agreed about that, though he thought it likely that it might be altered for them. There was no other way by which he could hope to get Juanita clear. But he shortened this talk because he was in a secret haste for the Inca to go. He thought that the time was near at which Jiros had said that he would withdraw the guard, and if it should happen while the Inca was still there, it might be hard to explain.

However, the Inca went while the guard remained, and Devereux was left to consider the new peril which Jiros's enmity must bring. For he saw that Jiros must have control of the escort rather than he (they would be men with whom he could have no speech!) and it would be hard indeed for him to win through, if Jiros had determined his death.

He saw that it would have been wiser, for himself, to stay where he was than to take the road of escape that Jiros had planned, but when he thought of Juanita he saw that there was no other way. Well, he would not be the first whom lust of treasure had brought to a soon death!

But the next event was as it had been planned. A messenger came to the guard, who readily took their orders to go. They went without sign of hesitation surprise, and Devereux thought that, after all, the escape might be made without suspicion, and the first, and perhaps the greatest danger be overcome. He could not know that, though the Inca was inclined to give him a doubtful trust, as Jiros's destined victim rather than his accomplice in any plot, yet he was leaving nothing to chance, and the guard had been three minutes withdrawn before he had been informed of what Jiros had done.

The Inca sat in his room, and Juanita and Kito were there. He had no design on Juanita's chastity at this hour though he kept her there in the night. Had all gone in a quiet way, his thoughts might have turned in a direction she would not have liked, yet even that is

186

a doubt, for after last night he was a sick man. What he had said now was: "You are my tongues, which I must have here for another need." So they waited there, and Juanita saw that the plan of escape was not likely to be for her.

CHAPTER THIRTY-FOUR

PRELUDE TO DEATH

DEVEREUX waited till the steps of the guard had echoed away, and a few minutes beyond and then began to pack as much as he could bear, having his rifle (but no ammunition beyond the cartridges it contained), and the sack of jewels, which was weight enough in itself for a moving man. He must also have the lamp in one hand, so that it was at a slow pace, and in poor array to face any danger that might arise, that he set along a passage that seemed silent and deserted enough.

He did not like the plan, which must keep him exposed to discovery and without possibility of escape for so long a time, and indefinitely after that if Jiros and Juanita should be delayed or prevented from coming, but it might be the best that Jiros could have contrived, and he supposed that he would keep faith with him until his use was done Indeed, he told himself with a resolute effort to see light on a black way, it was an advantage—it might be called a form of insurance to know the method by which his enemy planned his death. It must give him an easy mind toward others, by which it might have been mean at a nearer day.

So he thought as he went, but his reluctance was soon done, for he did not go far. He turned back, seeing soldiers that blocked the way. He had coolness enough when he saw them to stand in doubt at the corner to which he came, like a man lost and unsure, before he turned back to his own chamber, and when he arrived there he went for a short distance in the opposite direction, until he saw that that was also held by a strong guard, after which he went back, and laid his burdens down, to wait whatever might come.

He sat there for some time, while nothing happened, and meanwhile the time came at which Jiros should have brought Juanita to the water gate, which he would have done, for, to that point and beyond, he had intended to keep faith, as Devereux had supposed.

But when Jiros found that Juanita was in the Inca's rooms, he had a great fear for the position in which he stood, and a doubt what he should do, for it was a difficulty he had not foreseen.

He was a man who could be expected to think of himself only, but he was still far from understanding the extremity of his own peril, having no idea of the discovery of his mind which the Inca had made during the previous night. But he supposed that, if he should leave Devereux without warning of the fact that Juanita was unable to come, he would either attempt the passage alone, or else wait till he would be found by others at the coming of day, either of which events would have increased Jiros's perils, and wrecked his plans. So he determined to warn him of how matters stood.

He found Devereux in his own chamber, which he was glad to see, though the explanation he gave contained substance for anxious thought; and he was able to tell of where Juanita was with less trouble than he had expected to meet, as Devereux already knew that she was required for the Inca's use in another way from that which Jiros had in his thoughts.

As they talked, and before they had come to the forming of further plans, a messenger from the Inca stood at the chamber entrance.

He did reverence in a formal manner, and came in saying: "It is my speed that you are both here. The Inca cannot rest, and will have company in the night."

Jiros asked sharply: "Are many called?"

"There are about twelve."

"It is well," he said, in a relieved voice.

The messenger hurried on, and Jiros explained. "There is nothing strange in this, and it may be a good omen for us. There are many nights when his hand shakes and he cannot sleep, and he will then order a meal in his own room, and summon company of those whom the sun of his favour warms, that he may forget the loneliness of the night. If he tire, he will let us go, and if fortune be our friend at the last, we may still leave before dawn."

Devereux felt that this was a sanguine hope. He asked: "Was there a guard in the passage when you came?"

"No. There was none there."

"It is all a puzzle to me. But I think I see what I must do."

He loaded himself again, taking the rifle, the sack of stones, and all, excepting the lamp, as he had been burdened before.

Jiros asked: "Why do you do that?"

"I can answer that when the Inca tells you to ask."

So at this they went to the Inca's rooms, in one of which a banquet had been choicely spread for more than a dozen guests, among whom Juanita and Kito were set, though at the further end from where places for Jiros and Devereux were await.

The Inca seemed to be in a better mood than before, and when he observed how Devereux was laden, it was Jiros through whom he made enquiry of what it meant.

"Ask him," he said, "why he should come here less like a man than a huckster's mule?"

"It is because," Devereux replied, "I have this great trust that I cannot leave. I could have slept, had the guard stayed at the door, but when they withdrew I could neither let this wealth go far from my hand, nor could I rest till I had gone right and left to find that the guards were still there, though they had drawn further away. When I was summoned here, could I leave it alone? May it not all have been meant to test my prudence and care, with the greatest treasure that may ever have been in the hands of a single man?"

Jiros translated this well, as Devereux felt he could trust him to do. The Inca said: "So the guard withdrew, and he was troubled by that? Tell him I am conscious of all his care."

Jiros began: "The guard was—" But the Inca stopped him with: "If I would know, I will ask. For now, you may let it be." Jiros was puzzled, but content to have more time for an excuse it was not easy to frame.

A minute later he had a fresh occasion for fear, though it seemed that the Inca's lightning was not for him.

"You may say," the Inca ordered him, but in a smooth voice, as though talking of that which was known before, "where you have the water hidden away, for the Englishman cannot drink it at a better time."

Jiros had been in narrow passes before, and he was alert now to avoid surprise, but this was so unexpected a thing that it was hard to resolve at once in what manner it should be met. How should the Inca know that he had the water concealed? Or with what purpose it had been got? He could not guess, and he had no moment for

190

thought, but he saw that Devereux was condemned, and could only hope that he was not under the shadow of the same cloud. But it would be folly to deny what the Inca must surely know, for it must be something more than a random guess.

He rose: "I will go myself."

"No," the Inca replied, "I have one here who can go. It is too small a thing for you to make use of your own legs."

Jiros must say where it was, which he did, avoiding the fact that it was packed with some other things which would have been a load on his back now, had he been able to get away.

This conversation was not translated to Devereux, so that it had no meaning for him. It was all said in a quiet way. He saw that the storm delayed, but that lightning was overhead.

In a few minutes the messenger returned, and the gourd of water was in his hands.

The Inca said: "It is to the Lord Jiros that it belongs," and it was set before him where he sat with Devereux at his side.

Devereux guessed what it must be. He looked at Juanita at the other end of the board, and saw that her eyes were on it also, but as he looked they withdrew as though they would not show interest in a trivial thing. Well, she had warned him. What more was there that she could do?

Jiros understood what the Inca willed, and he did not delay. He poured out for himself, and for Devereux. He said: "This is good water, which take for my health's need. Will you drink with me?"

"I am not thirsty now. I will not rob you of what you need."

"Then I am sorry I asked," Jiros replied smoothly, "but I think you must do it now. For the eyes of others are on us, and it is against the custom of the land to refuse such an offered drink. They will construe it in a way that you do not mean."

"I mean nothing more than that I am not inclined to drink at this time. Surely a man may drink or not as he will?"

Devereux endeavoured to say this in a casual and friendly way, but he was annoyed to see that his hand was unsteady on the table beside the glass.

Jiros answered: "You are making trouble which both of us might avoid. Do you not see that the meal has paused, and that all eyes are upon us now? It is the Inca that you insult, and not me."

Devereux said: "I insult no one. Cannot a man drink as he will?"

It was true that all eyes were on him. Juanita's now, with a trouble they made no effort to hide. He saw that he was being invited to his own death, but what might be the end if he should refuse was harder to guess. He was so utterly in their power, and, except as Jiros might will, he could not even speak to them in his own defence.

"There is still time to be wise," Jiros said, "though it may not be long. See, I will drink myself. That should clear your doubt. Or will you change glasses with me?"

"I have heard of drinks which are good for those who are of the land, but which strangers should leave alone."

"Do you believe such nonsense as that? I tell you a truer thing. No one has yet guessed the way we chose for escape, and if you will be sensible now we may still get away by it before dawn; but, if you refuse to drink it will be the finish of all, and it is the girl's escape which you will prevent, as well as your own. I do not speak of myself, as I am so clearly one whom you do not trust."

Devereux considered this, and saw that, though Jiros was false, it might still be true. If the Inca's suspicions were directed only toward himself, he might be content when he saw him drink, thinking that his end would be sure. And it might still suit Jiros to get them away together. The water looked innocent enough. And who could say that he would not survive that which Jiros was able to drink? He remembered also that Peixoto had come through alive—at least long enough to regain civilised lands, which would be enough to make Juanita safe. He could not know that Peixoto had done no more than to wet his lips before having the cup struck from his hand.

He said: "Well, you shall have it your own way. It is too small a matter to stop the meal."

He raised the cup, and when he put it down he had drunk half it held, if not more. It tasted harmless enough. He heard a sigh from those who looked on, as though many breaths had been held and released at the same sign. He did not look at Juanita. "People die," he thought, "by their own fears, but I will go the opposite road. I must be well till we are clear of this place, and if they think I am doomed, and of no further account, it may be simpler to do."

It was a few minutes later that the Inca asked: "Is the moon-rise near?" And being told that it was already upon the edge of the world, he said: "Then we will visit the pit."

CHAPTER THIRTY-FIVE

SCREAMS IN THE NIGHT

THE order in which they moved would have made it difficult for them to speak, had either thought it to be a good moment for the attempt, but Devereux caught Juanita's eyes, and met them with a smile which was meant to show that hope and courage remained. She smiled faintly back, with a meaning he could not guess, but he saw that her face had become white with a fear that she could not hide.

They went through passages dimly lit by tray-shaped lamps on the walls: through galleries which Devereux had not previously seen: down stone stairs very many and shallow and wide, reminding him of pictures of Babylonian palaces, as it is imagined that they once were. They came at last to a rocky amphitheatre, open to the sky and the rising moon, with a large pool in its midst.

The Inca seated himself on a high throne carved from the rock. Those about him took lower seats which had been hewn out in the same way. Devereux became wonderingly aware that they were no longer few, but that guards were drawn up in long ranks to the right and left, and that crowds were dimly assembling below. On either side of the Inca's throne a trumpeter blew a high and lingering call. It was evident that this was to be something more than relief of the ennui of a wakeful night. He could only hope that they had finished with him, and that he was to take no further part in the play.

The moon rose, and its light increased. A broad lane of water silvered from shore to shore. The Inca's voice came clear and firm, as though he had been revived by the fresher air, or the excitement of what he did.

"Jiros," he said, "I will not ask you why the guard was withdrawn, or the water fetched, for you are one who is ever subtle to frame a lie. It is the beasts you shall tell in turn." And as he spoke, as though in answer to what he said, though it may have been no more than to welcome the spreading light, there came, frightful and shrill, the high screams that Devereux had heard during the nights before.

His eyes were becoming accustomed to the darkness now, which lessened as the moon rose. Dimly, he saw three ungainly, unmoving shapes, on the narrow edge of the lake. He thought: "They are the same creatures we saw before. They must have screamed then for the half-light of the storm."

But it was hard to believe. The screams were of an unearthly horror, as though they came from a far, primitive world, the creatures of which had plunged and jostled in steaming slime, before love or mercy began.

Kito said to Juanita: "They are those of which I told you before. The Inca means him to die. But it is not sure. They may be sluggish and let him go.... It is not often they move. The end one was just where it is now, more than a month ago."

"I wonder they can live, if they are as sluggish as that. How do they get food?"

"Oh, well, they are fed! And they are of a great age. But if they were not fed for three months, or perhaps six, it is said that they would become quicker to move, though it is what I have not seen.... There are others loose in the lake, but these are older than they, and are said to be very wise."

They watched Jiros the while she talked. He went down steps which would have been too narrow and steep for the giant toads to ascend, had they attempted such a strenuous climb. If he shook with fear, the moonlight was kind, as also that it hid his face, being at his side as he went down, and behind him as he advanced to the crouching toads.

He stood before the first, which even as it was squatting there was higher than he. He reached up a hand to put it upon a foul mouth, which was the price, if at all, at which his life might be won. He asked, in a voice that all who were assembled could hear: "Have I been faithful to him I serve?"

The toad took no notice of him at all. He withdrew his hand, and walked on to the next, to which he said the same words in the same way. It remained as still as a carved stone, and he may have been in a better hope as he went on to the third.

Here he repeated what he had asked before, and the toad did not move as he spoke, and it was only as he withdrew his hand, and must have thought that the game was won, that it spit out some venom with a great force and volume into his face. He fell at the creature's feet, being hard struck by the foul mess, and half sense-less and blind, and, as he fell, the toad moved a foot in a slow way, so that a toenail entered his side, holding him down.

They saw him, as his senses revived, struggle under the holding weight, but the toad did not appear to care whether he did that or lay still. His cries began and broke off abruptly, as though his lungs be-longed less to himself than the crushing toe.

Kito said: "It may eat him during the night, or he may be there in three days or four as he is now. It is said that they are skilful to hold their prey alive till they need a meal, and a week is not much to them."

The Inca rose. He was content with what he had done, but he was sick, and the trouble in his ears was worse than he had known it before.

He tried to see Devereux, and after some effort he focused his glance upon him, so that he saw that he still had the rifle and the sack of jewels which had been asking their price in blood, as they ever do. They were of small account to him, be he ill or well, having what he had. They could be put back on the next day.

He said: "You should go to your own room. You have seen jus-tice done. You will have some hours to observe your folly before you die."

Juanita looked at Kito, who had been a better friend to her than is yet said. She asked: "If I should return to my own land, would you come with me?"

Kito asked in turn: "Why should I do that? I should have no joy in a strange land."

"Your life would be safer than it is here."

"No. I would rather stay. I should lose too much."

Juanita saw that it would be useless to say more. Kito thought: "What should I do in her land? It would not be life. And she is not much more than beast. I saw hairs on her leg. And she will wed a savage who values stones."

On her own smooth body of olive-brown there was not a hair, however small, except on her head. They had been pulled out with care while she had been in her own land, and she had been taught to watch that they did not return. Animals have hairs, and the savage whites, who are like them in many ways. No. She would stay for a better fate in a better land....

Devereux went back to his own chamber. He felt dizzy and faint. He saw that the Inca had let him go in contempt, as being already dead. Well, had he done wrong, even so? Would he prefer to lie as Jiros was doing now?

Juanita entered. She was as burdened as he had been in the last hours. She said: "I must thank Jiros for one thing, that he showed me the way here, which I could not have asked or found. If you are ready, I think we cannot be too quick in getting away."

"If I can last," he said, "I will do all that I can."

"Why, do you think you are ill? There is no peril of that. Kito's brother changed the water at her request. She thought it would be safer for him, and might be much better for us, and it was what Jiros could never know he had done."

"Well, he has troubles enough, but I wish he could know it now. Why did you give me no hint? I have supposed I should be soon dead."

"Could I dare? It was the one chance that we had that no doubt should be breathed aloud. I was in a panic that you would not have the wisdom to drink. And after that I was afraid of my own eyes, lest they should give it away, till Kito told me what would be at the pool, for she knew not whom, and I think I was glad to shake with a real fear."

CHAPTER THIRTY-SIX

THE LAST OF JUANITA

A TALE may begin at a slow pace, and be forgiven for that, but it should end at a better speed.

It was for three months that they journeyed back, which would have been more had they not gone the way that the river moves, and it may be supposed that there were hardships they did not miss.

But they had few times that were more hard to endure than when they stood for two hours at the water gate while the passage drained, and waited in expectation at every moment that they would be found and their lives lost at the threshold of coming joy.

They had a much smaller doubt of the monster that they had seen when they had looked in from the other end, but, like most fears that are forethought, it was nought at last; for as the water had failed, the creature had fed full on fish and frogs that were left flopping upon the slime, so that when they came where it lay, it was in a doze, that would have made it a mere waste to use one of the bullets they had.

They entered Manaos without attracting notice of who they were, or being dogged by a public tale, and they travelled to Rio by different boats, as they, had planned that they would do while they had had time enough to both think and talk, when the paddle rested during the day, and perhaps a little for other things, concerning which, if we ask too far, we invite a lie.

It was in the upper lounge of the Hotel of the Seven Palms, looking down on the broad affluence of Avenida Avenue, that Devereux met a girl who had arrived nearly a week before, and whom it was hard for him to think he knew.

She asked: "I suppose your first thought will be to get back to England now?"

"It is what I should wish," he owned, "but if you feel that your life is here—I will tell you this. There was a time, shortly before we met, when I feared that I never could, for while I was here—in this hotel—less than a year ago, I heard that my firm had failed, and that I had lost all but what I had with me here…. Worse than that, I heard that my partner had been arrested for frauds in which it might be hard to prove that I had no part, and that I should certainly be invited to inhabit a jail while the truth were proved, which I had no inclination to do.

"I suppose now, that we are about the richest—"

"That you are."

"I said we. I suppose now, that that could be arranged, but if you say that your place is here, it is no more to give up than I supposed I had lost before."

"I think," she said, "before you decide, you should read this."

She handed him a newspaper of the date of two days before. He read, in a natural bewilderment, that Lady Phillida Lindhurst, who was reported to have been murdered with the whole of her uncle's expedition two years before, had—

"I tried," she said, "to keep it quiet, but it was not to be done. You will be pleased to see that the account which the reporters were good enough to make up for themselves is almost entirely wrong."

"But you said," he exclaimed. "You said Juanita was—"

"I said Juanita would do, and I think it did. I was not sure that I should ever be willing to let you know."

ABOUT THE AUTHOR

SYDNEY FOWLER WRIGHT (1874-1965) penned over seventy volumes of science fiction, fantasy, classic mysteries, historical novels, poetry, and non-fiction, many of them being published by the Borgo Press Imprint of Wildside Press.